DARK WORLD

DARK WORLD

Ghost Stories

Edited by
Timothy Parker Russell

With Stories by
Reggie Oliver, Christopher Fowler, Rhys Hughes,
Mark Valentine, Anna Taborska, John Gaskin,
Corinna Underwood, Rosalie Parker, Jason A. Wyckoff,
Mark J. Saxton, Jayaprakash Satyamurthy, R.B. Russell,
Stephen Holman and Steve Rasnic Tem

Tartarus Press

DARK WORLD
Edited by Timothy Parker Russell

First published by Tartarus Press, 2013 at
Coverley House, Carlton-in-Coverdale, Leyburn,
North Yorkshire, DL8 4AY, UK
www.tartaruspress.com

ISBN 978-1-905784-53-0

The editor and publishers would like to thank Barry and Susan Russell,
Janice Campbell, Stephen J. Clark, The Wensleydale School
and the authors for their support

'Mistake at the Monsoon Palace' by Christopher Fowler
was first published in *Red Gloves*, PS Publishing, 2011

Printed and bound by CPI Group (UK) Ltd, Croydon, CR0 4YY

300 copies of this first edition have been printed

129

All profits from the sale of this book go to
Amala Children's Home, India
www.amalatrust.org

CONTENTS

Life and death appeared to me ideal bounds, which I should first break through, and pour a torrent of light into our dark world.

Mary Wollstonecraft Shelley
Frankenstein; or the Modern Prometheus (1818)

INTRODUCTION
Timothy Parker Russell

All profits from this book will be used to help the Amala Children's Home, funding a three-week working trip in July 2013, and being donated directly to the cause. Located in the Tamil Nadu region of India, the home provides accommodation, food, safety and schooling for orphans and severely disadvantaged children. Without it, these children would be living on the streets of India, with all the immense hardships and dangers that brings.

I started thinking seriously about fundraising for Amala last September. A book seemed an excellent way of both raising money and producing something that those kind enough to donate could receive in return. I chose the ghost story theme primarily because I wanted this anthology to cross cultures—it is a genre that has been around since tales were first told, and is recognisable anywhere.

As evidence for that, I have had submissions from all over the world, and set all over the world. Included is an intriguing story from Jayaprakash Satyamurthy set in Bangalore and Dubai, and a beautiful tale from Christopher Fowler about an Indian palace. In Reggie Oliver's 'Come into My Parlour', horrors are closer to home, while Stephen Holman locates his unsettling story in a Los Angeles arts academy. Anna Taborska mixes old legends and the present day in Eastern Europe, and Mark Valentine sets his well-woven mystery somewhere in Northamptonshire. Rosalie Parker's 'Oracle' takes place in the Yorkshire Dales, for me much closer to home. It captures well the feel of the country-side—and how it can affect you.

I consider the term 'ghost story' to be a loose one. Ghosts come in many forms and very few of these stories could be considered 'conventional'—another reason for choosing this genre, and for why I love it. This has led to a very varied collection of haunted stories.

It only remains for me to thank you for buying this book, and I hope you enjoy it. I am very grateful, but more importantly so are the many children that benefit from the Amala Children's Home. If you want to know more about the project or help further, please visit www.amalatrust.org.

COME INTO MY PARLOUR
Reggie Oliver

'Will you walk into my parlour?' said the Spider to the Fly,
' 'Tis the prettiest little parlour that ever you did spy;
The way into my parlour is up a winding stair,
And I've a many curious things to shew when you are there.'

From *The Spider and the Fly* by
Mary Howitt (1799-1888)

Somehow I always knew that there was a problem with Aunt Harriet.

She was my father's only sister—step-sister, as it happens—and older than he was by eleven years. She was unmarried and her work was something to do with libraries: that much was clear, but the rest was rather a mystery. She lived in a small flat near Victoria Station in London which we heard about but never saw, but she often used to come to stay with us—rather *too* often for my mother's taste. In fact, the only time I ever remember my parents 'having words', as we used to say, was over Aunt Harriet yet again coming down for the weekend.

'Yes, I know, I know, dear,' I heard my father say. 'But I can't exactly refuse her. She is my sister.'

'Exactly,' said my mother. 'She's only your sister. You *can* say no to her occasionally.'

But apparently my father couldn't. Fortunately she did only stay for weekends, that is apart from Christmas, but I'll come to that later.

Dark World

At that time we lived in Kent and my father commuted into London by train every weekday morning. Where we lived was semi-rural; there were places to walk and wander: there were woods and fields nearby. I like to think that my younger sister and I had a rather wonderful childhood; if it were not for Aunt Harriet.

Am I exaggerating her importance? It is a long time ago now, but I rather think I'm not. I suspect that she loomed even larger then than she does in my memory.

She was a big, shapeless woman who always seemed to be wearing several layers of clothing, whatever the weather. She dyed her hair a sort of reddish colour and rattled a little from the various bits of jewellery she had about her. (She was particularly fond of amber.) Her nose was beaky and she carried with her everywhere an enormous handbag, the contents of which remained unknown.

When she came she brought with her an atmosphere of unease and discontent. She never allowed herself to fit in with us. If we wanted to go for a walk, she would stay behind. If we decided to stay indoors, she would feel like going out. She rarely took part in any game or expedition we had planned, and when she did there was always a fault to find with the arrangements. On the other hand, almost invariably she wanted, often at the most inconvenient times, to 'have a talk' as she put it, with my father. He never refused her demands and so they would go into his study, often for several hours, to have their talk.

I once asked my mother what it was all about.

'They're probably discussing the Trust,' she said.

I never really understood this Trust. I once asked my father about it but he refused to reveal anything. Many years later, after my father's death, I searched among his papers for evidence of it and could find nothing. The little I knew came at second-hand from my mother. She said that some distant relation had left a sum of money jointly to my father and Aunt Harriet, and Aunt Harriet was always trying to get more income from it, or do something mysterious called 'breaking the Trust' so that she could extract a lump sum for her personal use.

I don't think my aunt ever really cared about my sister and me as people, but she would ask us the kind of questions that grown-ups tend to ask: questions that are almost impossible to answer. 'How are you getting on at school?' 'Have you made any nice friends there?' I don't think she would have been interested in our answers even if they had been less boring and evasive than the ones we gave her.

Mealtimes were especially grim. In the first place Aunt Harriet was a vegetarian and my mother, out of courtesy I suppose, insisted that we were also vegetarian during her stays. That meant doing without a Sunday roast, which we resented. My mother was not a great cook at the best of times, but she was particularly uninspired in her meatless dishes. Then, during the meal, Aunt Harriet would either be silent in such a way as to discourage conversation from us, or indulge in long monologues about office politics in the library service. This always struck us—that is, my sister and me, and probably my parents too—as horribly boring. We gathered from her talk that work colleagues were always trying, as she said, 'to put one over' on her, and she was always defeating them.

In spite of this, you may be surprised to know, I came to be fascinated by her. I suppose it was because she was, at the same time, such a big part of our lives, and yet so remote. Her life in London, apart from those dreary office politics, was a closed book. She never talked about going to theatres or concerts or exhibitions or watching sport. She didn't even really talk about books. She never mentioned any friends. It was this mystery about her that started all the trouble.

It began, I suppose, one Sunday in September when I was nine, and Aunt Harriet was then approaching sixty. We had just finished lunch and the meal had not pleased Aunt Harriet. It had been, if I remember rightly, cauliflower cheese, not one of my mother's cooking triumphs admittedly, but perfectly edible. My Aunt's complaint had been that my mother should have made an effort to supply something more original from the vegetarian repertoire.

She began: 'I'm not complaining, but—' a disclaimer which, paradoxically, often prefaced her complaints '—I'm just saying. You might occasionally like to take a look in a vegetarian cook book for your own benefit. Of course I don't mind; I'm just your sister-in-law, but if you were to have guests here, important guests—of course I know I'm not important—and they happened to be vegetarian—'

At this point my father, usually the most patient of men, exploded. He could put up with a lot of things but this was not to be borne, especially as it involved my mother, whom he adored. Even so, it was a brief explosion, and fairly reasonably expressed.

'Oh, for heavens sake, stop talking nonsense, Harriet!' he said, not in his usual quiet voice.

My aunt sniffed, rose from the table and announced that she had never been so insulted in her life and was going for a walk. She then quitted the dining room and a few seconds later we heard the door bang. We ate the rest of the meal in virtual silence.

After lunch my curiosity got the better of me. It was a damp, dull sort of day, so the prospect of going out was not inviting, even without the possibility of meeting Aunt Harriet, sullen faced, tramping about the countryside. I decided that this was my moment for exploring her room and seeing if I could find any clues to her bizarre behaviour.

There was one spare bedroom in the house for guests, and because few occupied it but she, it was known as Harriet's Room. She stayed there most weekends in the year and, though the furnishings of the room were very impersonal she had somehow made the place her own.

First of all, there was the smell. It wasn't an unpleasant smell in itself, but because it was from the perfume she wore it had dark associations. It was musky, spicy, not exactly unclean but somehow not fresh. The atmosphere was heavy with it because, with typical disregard for my parents' heating bills, she had left the bar of an electric fire on in her room.

The dressing table was crowded with an assortment of bottles of unguents and medicines. Aunt Harriet was, in her quiet way, a hypochondriac, always suffering from some kind of affliction from heart palpitations to boils.

On the dressing table were also a number of black lacquer boxes, some rather beautiful, either painted or decorated with inlaid mother-of-pearl. Tentatively, and knowing that now I was somehow crossing a line, I opened one box, then another, then another.

They all contained jewellery or trinkets, the stones semi-precious and mostly made out of her beloved amber. Many were in the shape of animals or strange beasts of mythical origin. One in particular intrigued me. It sat on a bed of cotton wool in a small box of its own. The box was black like the others with a scene painted in gold on the top in the Japanese style of cranes flying over a lake bordered by waving reeds. The thing inside this box was carved out of amber, a dark, translucent reddish-brown, smooth and polished to perfection. It appeared to be an insect of some kind, perhaps a beetle or spider with a bloated body and eight strange little stumpy legs of the kind you see on caterpillars. The workmanship was extremely fine and, as I now think, Japanese, like the box. Its head was round and dome-like with two protruding eyes almost complete spheres emerging from the middle of the head. Into these amber eyes the carver had managed to insert two tiny black dots which gave them a kind of life and, somehow, malignity. He (or she?) had carved the mouth parts to give an impression of sharp, predatory teeth—or whatever it is that insects have instead of teeth. It was beautifully made, and horrible. I shut the box quickly.

I turned my attention to the bedside table. It was piled high with books, mostly old and somewhat battered, but some finely bound. I noticed that many of the bindings had little square discolourations as if a label had been removed from their surfaces. I wondered if my aunt had brought them here to read because they were an odd selection. There was an early nineteenth-century treatise on metallurgy, a volume on alpine plants by a Victorian clergyman with some fine colour plates, a few modern novels in their original dust jackets and several children's books. Besides these books I noticed a small plain wooden box, this time not containing trinkets but a neat set of small brushes, a needle-sharp scalpel knife, two pairs of tweezers and small square glass bottles containing fluids such as ink eradicator. I was puzzling over this mysterious collection when I heard someone behind me.

'What are you doing in my room, little man?'

I think I jumped several feet into the air in my fright. I had been sitting on the bed facing away from the door and Aunt Harriet had crept in unnoticed. The next moment she had me by the ear.

'I asked you what you were doing. Well . . . ?'

It was some moments before I was sufficiently in control to reply.

'Just looking.'

'Looking? Looking for what?'

'I don't know.'

'Do you make a habit of snooping around the rooms of your parents' guests?'

'No!'

'Oh, so you think it's all right to snoop around in *my* room. Is that it?'

'No! Let me go!' She had not released my ear.

'What do you think your father would say if I said I found you in my room trying to steal my things? Mmm?'

'I wasn't stealing anything! You won't tell him, will you?' I was not afraid of my father as such—he was not a fierce man—but I was afraid of disappointing him. At last Aunt Harriet began to relax her grip on my ear, but she had left it throbbing and painful, full of the blood of embarrassment.

'We shall have to see about that. I *may* not have to tell him,' said Aunt Harriet in a softer, almost caressing voice which was, however, no more reassuring. 'It all depends on whether you're going to be a helpful boy to me. Are you going to be a helpful boy, or a nasty, spiteful, sneaking boy?'

'Helpful,' I said, instantly dreading the menial task she would almost certainly set me.

'So I should think. All I'm going to ask is something really quite simple—' Suddenly she looked alarmed and turned round. My six year old sister Louise had wandered in and was standing in the doorway, her wide blue eyes staring at us in amazement. She had pale golden curls in those days and looked the picture of innocence, but evidently not to my aunt.

7

'Run away, little munchkin,' she said. 'Can't you see I'm talking to your grown-up brother?' Louise had never been called a 'munchkin' before. She probably didn't know what it meant—neither did I, for that matter—but it sounded cruel from my aunt's lips so she burst into tears. Aunt Harriet stared at her in astonishment. She obviously had no idea why she had provoked such a reaction. After Louise had run off, still wailing, to find my mother, my Aunt said: 'That child has been dreadfully spoilt.'

I felt that it was my turn to leave so I started to shuffle towards the door. Aunt Harriet hauled me back by the ear again.

'Hold hard, young Lochinvar. Where do you think you're going? I haven't told you what I want you to do, yet, have I?'

'You can do it later, Aunt Harriet.'

'Later won't do. Later will never do.' Then she told me what she wanted. At some time during the week I was to go into my father's study and from the second drawer down on the left hand side of my father's kneehole desk I was to extract a blue folder labelled FAMILY TRUST. I was then to place it under the mattress in my Aunt's room so that when she came the following weekend she might study it at her leisure.

It was a simple task, but it terrified me. I didn't know which was worse: to defy my aunt or to betray my father. I was going back to school shortly so I decided to postpone any decision and hope that Aunt Harriet would have forgotten all about it by the time she came next. That, of course, was a vain hope.

When she came the following weekend I avoided her as much as I could until finally she caught me early on Sunday morning as I was passing her door on the way to the bathroom. She dragged me inside and closed the door. She was strong for her age and build.

'Where is it?' She hissed into my face. She wore a Chinese silk dressing gown covered in dragons over a red flannel night-dress.

'Where's what?'

'Don't you play games with me, little man. You know perfectly well what I wanted. Why didn't you get it for me?'

'I couldn't,' I extemporised. 'The drawer was locked.'

'Little liar!' She said. 'I've seen your father open that drawer a thousand times and never once has he used a key. Dear God, can't you do just one simple little thing for me?'

'Why can't you get it yourself?'

'Because I can't. Never you mind. Because I need you to prove to me that you're not a nasty sneaking little boy, but someone who is loyal and will do his aunt a small favour. I am very disappointed with you. As a matter of fact, I was planning a little treat for you if you had succeeded. I was going to invite you up to London like a proper grown-up guest, and I would have given you tea in the Victoria Hotel with toasted tea cakes covered in butter and taken you to see a pantomime, and the Victoria and Albert Museum and shown you the beautiful and valuable things in my home. You'd have liked that. You like nosing into other people's property, don't you? But now you'll never have any of that because you won't do a simple thing for your poor old aunt.' She paused for breath and studied me closely. She could see I was unimpressed.

'Do you know what is going to happen to you if you don't do as I say?' She said, putting her face so close to mine our noses almost touched.

'No,' I said. Then, suddenly feeling that she was engaged in a game of bluff, I added: 'And I don't care.'

'Don't care, eh?' She said withdrawing her face and studying me intently. 'Don't care was made to care. I want to see that file by Christmas, or else. . . .'

'Or else what?'

Aunt Harriet once again put her huge old face very close to mine. I was almost overwhelmed by her musky perfume. In a loud croaking whisper, she said: ' "I can show you fear in a handful of dust." Do you know who said that?'

I shook my head.

'A very famous poet called Tom Eliot. I knew him once: rather well, actually. He was very much in love with me at one time. A great many famous men were in love with me in those days, you know.'

I found this impossible to believe then, but years later when I was going through my late father's things I found a single photograph of Aunt Harriet as a young woman in the mid 1930s. It was a studio portrait and she was posed, rather artificially, elbow on knee, face cupped in her palm, staring at the camera. She wore a long double rope of pearls knotted in the middle as was the fashion and a loose rather 'arty' dress. Her dark shiny hair was cut in a page boy bob which framed a perfectly oval face, like one of Modigliani's women. Below the fringe of hair her big dark eyes had allure. You might well have described her as attractive; you might also have said that the hungry look in her eyes and the sulky, sensual mouth signalled danger.

'I can show you fear in a spider's web,' she said. 'Do you know who said that?'

Again I shook my head.

'I did. And I can too. So beware, my young friend. Beware!'

With that I was dismissed. I was inclined to regard her threats as empty, or rather that is what I wanted to believe.

In the months running up to Christmas she came, much to our relief, less frequently at weekends, but when she did she always found an opportunity to get me on my own. Then she would ask one question: 'Have you got it yet?' I would shake my head and that would be that, or so I thought. She seemed strangely untroubled by my refusal to co-operate. Then came Christmas.

She always spent several days with us over Christmas, arriving on Christmas Eve and occasionally lingering until New Year's Day. Her presence was not so annoying as it might have been because my parents were hospitable during the season. In the company of people other than family Aunt Harriet would occasionally make an effort to be pleasant, provided that she felt that the guests were not beneath her notice socially. It was the one time too when my mother would not make any concessions to my aunt's vegetarian diet, simply feeding her with the vegetables that dressed the turkey.

Aunt Harriet came that Christmas Eve, as usual with great fuss and circumstance. She did not drive, so my father had to fetch her from the station in the car. It was dark when she arrived at our house and a light snow was falling, the little specks of white dancing in the wind. I remember looking out of the window of our house as her vast black bulk squeezed itself out of our car and onto the drive. She seemed to regard the snow as a personal annoyance, and flapped her hand in front of her face to brush away the flakes, as if they were stinging insects. As she lumbered towards the front door my father was busy getting her suitcases and parcels out of the boot.

I knew about these parcels from previous Christmases. They were all very grandly wrapped and decked out with tinsel and fancy ribbons, but they never contained anything anyone really wanted. To my father she gave cigars which he very rarely smoked; and to my mother, almost invariably, a Poinsettia plant with its piercingly red and green foliage.

I once heard my mother say to my father: 'Doesn't she know I hate Poinsettias? Nasty gaudy plants. They look like cheap Christmas decorations. Ugh!'

'Why don't you tell her?' said my father smiling.

'Good grief, no! Can you imagine the scene she'd make?' And they both laughed.

Louise and I always got books, but they were hardly ever new ones, and never what we actually wanted. Some of them, I now think, were probably quite valuable, but even that was a cheat, as I'll explain later.

My mother, Louise and I were lined up in the hall, as usual, to greet her. When she got to me she murmured: 'have you got it?' I shook my head. She sort of smiled and pinched my cheek in a would-be friendly manner, but she pinched so hard that my face was red and sore for quite some time afterwards. I had a feeling that there was worse to come.

Christmas passed off much as usual. Aunt Harriet refused to come to church, saying that she worshipped God in her own way, whatever that meant, and that anyway the whole business of Christmas was just a debased and commercialised pagan ceremony. When the turkey was being carved she insisted on referring to it loudly as 'the bird corpse'. It was no better and no worse than usual. Then, after the dinner, came the present giving.

My father got his usual cigars and my mother her hated Poinsettia. I forget what Louise received, but I certainly remember my present. It felt heavy inside its red and gold Christmas paper.

When I unwrapped it I found, not much to my surprise, that it was a book. Of its kind it was rather a sumptuous volume, bound in green artificial leather, heavily embossed with gold. It was in astonishingly good condition considering that the date on its title page was 1866. The pages were thick and creamy, their edges gilded. I noted that the book was illustrated throughout: 'drawn', as the title page announced 'by eminent artists and engraved by the brothers Dalziel'. All this might have attracted me, but for the title of the book itself:

A CHILD'S TREASURY OF INSTRUCTIVE
AND IMPROVING VERSE

I did not like that at all. Now, I was nine at the time, but I already considered myself a young adult, not a child. Louise, at six, was still a child, not me. I read quite grown-up books like Sherlock Holmes, and *Treasure Island*, and *The Lord of the Rings*. Moreover, I did not want to be instructed and improved: I got quite enough of that at school, thank you. I felt the first sting of Aunt Harriet's revenge for my failure to do as she had told me. Then I looked at the fly-leaf.

It was not quite as smooth as the other pages. It was slightly buckled and looked as if it had been treated with some kind of bleach. On it Aunt Harriet had written in purple ink: 'to Robert. Happy Christmas from Aunt Harriet.' Then, in smaller writing a little further down the page she had written: 'p256.'

When I thanked Aunt Harriet for her present with a rather obvious lack of enthusiasm, she merely smiled and tried to pinch my cheek again, but I avoided her. 'It's a very precious book,' she said. 'I think you'll find it interesting.'

'Oh, it's beautiful,' said my mother, for once backing up my aunt. 'Those wonderful Dalziel engravings. They were the best, weren't they? And such perfect condition! Where did you find it, Harriet?'

Aunt Harriet gave my mother a dark look, as if she suspected some kind of insinuation in her question. Then, seeing that my mother was, as always, being innocently straightforward, she smiled. 'I have my methods,' she said.

Later that night when I was in bed I began to ponder over Aunt Harriet's present and that cryptic little note, so I got the book and turned to page 256. It was a poem entitled 'The Spider and the Fly' by someone called Mary Howitt.

> 'Will you walk into my parlour?' said the Spider to the Fly,
> ' 'Tis the prettiest little parlour that ever you did spy;
> The way into my parlour is up a winding stair,
> And I've a many curious things to shew when you are there.'
> 'Oh no, no,' said the little Fly, 'to ask me is in vain,
> For who goes up your winding stair can ne'er come down
>   again.'

At the time I wasn't much into poetry and this was really not my thing at all, but the verse had an oddly compelling quality. I somehow had to read on. There was this ridiculous conversation going on between a spider and a fly—as if two insects could talk! —and the spider was enticing the fly into her den and the fly was, so far, refusing. It was so strange, this weird blend of insect and human life, like a dream, that I was held. I turned the page.

It was then that I got a shock. I was confronted with a black and white engraving. It showed a creature standing in front of a cleft in a rock with the winding stair within going up into the darkness. I say 'a creature' because it was half human half spider, and it appeared to me to be a 'she', mainly because the head bore a quite shocking resemblance to Aunt Harriet. There was the same longish nose and wide shapeless mouth; above all the bulging eyes had the same predatory stare. The head was fixed, without a neck, onto a great bloated, bulbous body, again rather like Aunt Harriet's. From the base of this sprang two long, thin legs that sagged at the knee joints as if the great body was too heavy to be held upright. From the body—or thorax, I suppose—came four almost equally thin arms, two from each side. The muscles on the arms were as tight and wiry as whip-cord, and what passed for hands at their extremities were more like crabs' pincers and looked as if they could inflict terrible pain.

Standing in front of this monstrous creature, its back to the viewer, was what I assumed was the fly, though it barely resembled one. It looked more like a very tall thin young Victorian dandy. Its wings were folded to form a swallow tailed coat, one thin arm rested on a tasselled cane and a top hat was set at a jaunty angle on top of its small head. It looked a feeble, doomed creature.

The picture and the poem seemed to me all of a piece, at once surreal and yet frighteningly vivid, inhabiting a world of its own, full of savage, predatory monsters and enfeebled victims. I read on until the inevitable ending.

With buzzing wings he hung aloft, then near and nearer drew,
Thinking only of his brilliant eyes, and green and purple hue—
Thinking only of his crested head—poor foolish thing! At last,
Up jumped the cunning Spider, and fiercely held him fast.
She dragged him up her winding stair, into her dismal den,
Within her little parlour—but he ne'er came out again!

There were some moralising lines after that, something about 'to idle, silly flattering words, I pray you ne'er give heed'. But that was just a piece of nonsense put in to give the poem respectability. It was the image that remained, and the torturing fear of being seized and carried up a winding stair into the darkness.

I barely slept that night, and when I did it was worse than being awake. Waking or sleeping there was the sense that something was in one corner of my room. I saw it—if I saw it at all—only on the edge of my vision, and not when I looked at it directly: a bloated thing with a head but no neck, and with several arms or legs that waved at me in a slow way, like a creature at the bottom of the sea. This torment lasted until the frosty dawn when light began to filter through my thin window curtains. At last I managed some untroubled sleep until, hardly two hours later, I was summoned down to breakfast.

On Boxing Day afternoon my parents had a party for neighbours and their children. Aunt Harriet was less than enthusiastic about the affair and went out for a walk immediately after lunch so as not to involve herself in the preparations. On her return, just as a cold sallow sun was setting, the party had begun. She sat among the guests in the sitting room sipping tea and smiling on the proceedings as if she were a specially honoured guest. Occasionally she would condescend to talk to some of our older friends. Various games were organised for the children who came, including Hide and Seek. When this was proposed Aunt Harriet beckoned me over and said: 'I give you permission to hide in my room. They'll never find you there.'

The idea did not appeal to me at all, but it stayed in my head. Those of us who were to hide began to disperse about the house and I remember finding myself in the passage outside my aunt's room. It was a moment when the temptation to enter her room seemed unconquerable as I heard the numbers being counted inexorably down to one in the hallway below. I entered her room.

I did not turn the light on. The room was warm and had that familiar musky smell. In the dim light I felt my way across to a walk-in cupboard which I entered and then shut behind me. I was now in utter darkness and silence. The noise and bustle of the house had vanished and the only sensation to which I was alive was that of touch. As I sat down on the floor of the cupboard my face was brushed by the soft cool tickle of my Aunt Harriet's fur coat. How did she reconcile the possession of this article with her vegetarianism? That was a question that only occurred to me long years later.

At first I felt a curious exhilaration. I was alone, unseen and quiet. I had myself to myself and no-one would break in on my solitude for a long while. I was free of the importunings of my little sister or the more serious demands of my parents. Moreover, the house, heated generously for once by central heating, Christmas candles and company had become a little stuffy. In here it was exquisitely cool. I allowed my undistracted thoughts to slow to a standstill; I may even have fallen asleep.

Darkness is a strange thing: it is both infinite and confining: it holds you tight in its grasp, but it holds you suspended in a void. Silence operates in a similar way. Slowly, the two combine to become a threat. I had no idea how much time had passed before I began to feel that it was time that someone found me, but how could they? I was so well hidden. It was then that I decided to open the cupboard door and let myself out. But it would not open.

My heart's thumping was suddenly the loudest noise in the universe. I was trapped forever in darkness and silence. I banged and kicked at the cupboard door, but to no effect. It seemed to have the strange unyielding hardness of a wall rather than a piece of wood. I shouted as loud as I could, but my voice was curiously close and dead as if I had entered a soundproof studio at midnight.

It was then that I became aware that the space I was in was not entirely dark. Yet, I was confused because, though I knew the cupboard I was in to be about three feet by six feet square the light that I saw seemed to be coming from a great distance. It was an indeterminate blue-green in colour, a rather drab hue, I thought. I stretched out my hand towards it in the hope of touching the back of the cupboard, but I felt nothing but the faintest brush of cold air, as if someone were blowing on my hand from beyond my reach.

By this time I had no sense of where the front, or the back, or the sides of the cupboard were. All appeared to be beyond my reach, and when I felt upwards I could not even sense the cold softness of my aunt's fur coat. Moreover the floor began to feel icy and damp. I stood up. Nothing now existed but the distant blue green light.

The next thing that happened was that the light began to grow. The difficulty was that I could not be sure whether I was moving towards it or it towards me. All I knew was that with each move, the atmosphere became more icy, as if I had been transported out of doors into an Arctic void.

The light began to assume shape, and I started to sense that it was a luminous object that was moving towards me. It came not steadily but in little fits or scuttlings. The thing had six legs or arms and a bulbous body that glowed. The head, smaller but equally round was darker, though the eyes shone. Their colour was reddish, like amber. It came on and my own body became paralysed with fear, so that I could not retreat from it.

The eyes fixed themselves on me. I tried to raise my hands and found them confined by some fibrous substance, heavy and sticky. In an imitation of my movement the creature stopped and raised two of its forelimbs in the air and began to wave them in front of its face. It appeared to be in the act of communicating with someone or something, but not with me. Then with a sudden leap it was on me and its sinewy, fibrous legs were pawing at my face. I cried out and fell, and when I opened my eyes again I found that I had fallen out of the cupboard into my aunt's room. I was covered in cobwebs.

When I emerged from her room the house was quiet and for a moment I thought it was deserted, but a faint sound from below reassured me. When I came downstairs, I found that my parents, Aunt Harriet and Louise were there, but all our guests had gone. I was chided for having fallen asleep in my hiding place. My Aunt Harriet smiled, but my mother was looking anxiously at me.

'You're shivering,' she said. 'You must be sickening for something. Come along. Off to bed with you.'

I was told later that it was flu of some sort and quite serious, but I remember virtually nothing about the next few days. Fortunately none of the others in the house caught my influenza and Aunt Harriet went home early to avoid infection. When I had recovered some sort of consciousness and was beginning to convalesce I asked for some books to read. I noticed that the ones provided did not include *A Child's Treasury of Instructive and Improving Verse*. I asked after it but was told by my mother that she had burned it in the garden. In the delirium of my fever I had talked about it endlessly, and with apparent terror. 'And when I looked in it, I could see why. There were the most beastly illustrations in it. Beautifully done, but beastly.'

'What sort of things?'

'I don't know . . . hobgoblins and demons, and . . . all sorts of horrid things.'

'But why did you have to burn it?'

'Oh, I had a book like that when I was a girl. It caused no end of trouble,' she said, and that was all she would say.

Some weeks later news reached us that Aunt Harriet had died. She had been crossing a busy road near her flat in Victoria

late at night and a car had hit her and she had had some sort of
heart seizure from which she never recovered. The details are
vague in my mind and I have never sought clarity by looking at
her death certificate. It is enough to say that in death she was as
much trouble as she was in life. It transpired that shortly before
that Christmas when she last came to us she had been dismissed
from her job in the library service. There were allegations about
missing books which were never fully resolved and my parents
had to satisfy the authorities that we did not have any stolen
books in our possession, nor had we profited from their illegal
sale.

With the exception of a small bequest to an obscure animal
charity Aunt Harriet had left everything of which she died
possessed to my father. There came a time when both my
parents had to go up for a few days to deal with the sale of my
Aunt's flat and its contents. I begged to be allowed to come with
them and help but they firmly refused, so Louise and I were left
at home in the care of a neighbour. On their return my parents
looked exhausted and somehow haunted. It was only a few
months later that my father began to show signs of the illness
that later took his life.

Deprived of a sight of it myself I begged my father and
mother for details of what they had found in Aunt Harriet's flat,
but they were not forthcoming. My father simply would not
discuss it, and all my mother said was:

'You wouldn't have liked it. It's a horrible place. There were
cobwebs everywhere.'

MISTAKE AT THE
MONSOON PALACE
Christopher Fowler

'Iska kyadaam hal?'
'How much does this cost?'
Marion Wilson gave up trying to memorise the phrases. She looked up from her guidebook, switching her attention to the driver. 'Sorry, what did you say?'

'I said my cousin owns the best pashmina shop in Jaipur,' Shere told her. 'He will be honoured to make you a special deal because you are my valued client.'

Sure, she thought, *this guy is your cousin, your* brother, *your uncle, anyone other than some creep you cut deals with to rob rich, gullible Americans.* She impatiently tapped the guidebook with her forefinger, recalling the page about touts and conmen.

'I assure you, you will not find finer materials in all of India.'

'Forget it, Shere, it's not going to happen,' she told him. 'Trust me, I bought enough stuff yesterday to fill an extra suit-case.' In the three days that Shere had been appointed as her driver, they had visited jewellery stores selling silver bracelets that broke in half the first time you wore them, 'hand-woven' scarves produced by children in a Mumbai sweatshop and wooden statues of Ganesh that looked like they'd been speed-carved in the dark. 'Let's get on, it's already ten.'

'But Madam, this shop is of highest quality, government approved, everyone goes there, Richard Gere, everyone.' The

21

driver was wobbling his head amiably. 'We stop for five minutes, no longer, and you do not have to buy if you do not wish.'

'Well, I do *not* wish.' She pulled a small plastic bottle of antiseptic wash from her trousers and poured a little of the blue liquid into her hands. She had been touching rupees so soft and brown that they looked as if they'd been used for—she dreaded to think what. She silently repeated the hygiene rule; right hand for taking money and greeting, because here the left hand was used as a substitute for toilet paper. Not that she was as pernickety as some. Iris, her companion from Ohio, had arrived in Delhi with an entire suitcase full of bottled water, which was taking things a little too far.

The little white taxi nosed its way back out of the crowded market square toward the main road, a dusty two-lane highway filled with overladen trucks, hay carts and sleeping cows. It was the end of the first week in July, and the monsoon season had yet to start, but the sky was dark with sinister cumulus. The ever-present pink mists that softened the views in every town they had visited had gone now, to be replaced by hot clear stillness. Marion wanted to open the window, to breathe something other than filtered freezing air, but could see black clouds of mosquitoes rising from ditches of dead water as the car passed.

Her attention drifted back to the guide book, which had fallen open on a list of Indian gods. The text was accompanied by tiny pastel drawings which made them all look the same. Bhairav. Ganesha. Hanuman. Rama. Shiva. Surya. Vishnu. Arrayed in lilac and yellow, blue and pink they rode birds, bore swords, cups, fire, tridents and bows, a vast network of deities who still seemed to hold some kind of power over the lives of ordinary people . . . she felt her eyes closing as the car swayed, and saw for a moment a bejewelled god lit by a curved prism of rubies and sapphires, spangling and spinning from his head. Feeling faint, she blinked the colours away.

She glanced up to the scenes rolling beyond the glass. Azure, crimson and sunflower bolts of cloth were stacked on the dirty pavement like a disassembled rainbow. The traffic was detouring around a buffalo that stood in the middle of the road, patiently chewing a plastic bag. It wore a gold-trimmed dress, its horns painted blue, its pierced ears laced with bells.

An ancient, bony man in a pink turban was squatting on the hard shoulder, cooking a chicken over an upright burning tyre.

A motorised rickshaw overtook them with two children and a piebald goat wedged inside it.

An elephant driver was asleep in a faded red *houdah*, waiting for tourist coaches that would not arrive—the latest wave of terrorist bombings had seen to that. A wedding band in yellow and silver uniforms were wearily donning the jackets they had dried on a row of thorn bushes.

A quartet of girls in identical yellow saris walked by, all listening to the same song on their mobile phones.

What do they think when they see me? Marion thought. *Do they even see me? Am I as invisible to them as they are in my country?*

What she first thought was a sparkling blue lake turned out to be a great ditch filled with empty plastic bottles.

'Where you want to go now?' the driver asked. Marion looked down at the guidebook in her lap and squinted at endless pages of forts and markets. Despite the low temperature in the vehicle, she felt overheated and fractious. She was still angry with Iris for deserting her five days into the trip. A few bouts of diarrhoea and she was calling her husband, making arrangements to return home. The secret was to keep tackling the spicy food until your stomach adjusted, Marion had been told. *You've an iron constitution,* her father had always said, *you're made of stronger stuff than your mother. You just have too much imagination.*

The driver had pulled the car over to the side of the road, and was talking to two young men with old faces, nondescript Indians of the type you saw everywhere, skinny and serious to the point of appearing mournful, with side partings and brown sweaters and baggy suit trousers hiding thin legs. Most of the men seemed to do nothing but sit around drinking *chai* while the women wielded pick-axes in rubble-filled vacant lots.

She tried to listen in on the conversation but realised they were speaking Hindi. 'Who are these people?' she asked, leaning forward between the headrests.

'My brothers. They would like to get a lift. It is not far to their town.'

'I met your brothers three days ago, Shere, and these are not the same guys. You think everyone looks the same to foreigners? They don't, not anymore. Those days are over. These guys are not your brothers and cannot come in the car, it's out of the question. Besides, I thought we had to get to Jodhpur?'

'That is tomorrow. Today you may choose where you would like to go.'

To be honest, she was not entirely sure where they were going next. Everything on the itinerary sounded the same. She had picked it from four others on her travel agent's website. According to the schedule, she was staying in an old Maharajah's palace, a vast amber fortress that looked like a child's sandcastle in the photograph, now converted into a luxury hotel. She was tired of eating in ornate, deserted dining rooms. The only other tourists she had seen on the entire trip were a pair of elderly British ladies who seemed to be duplicating her trip town by town. Their reasons for coming to India mystified her, because she often overheard them sharply asking the waiters for poached eggs or sausages and toast, anything but Indian food.

She studied the arguing men from the window. Perhaps they were really his brothers. Everything here was designed to confuse, and everyone, it seemed had the same first impressions; the colours, the mess, the filth, the lost grandeur, the blurred light, the beautiful children . . . part of her wanted to explore the narrow backstreets alone, but the touts and beggars were simply too exhausting, and Shere insisted on remaining by her side wherever she went. It was clearly considered too dangerous to let tourists explore for themselves. It seemed that they had to be brought in and unloaded, like boats being towed to docks.

But oh, the children. Tiny boys with withered feet or hands, dragging themselves along the central reservation of the road on little carts, kohl-eyed girls balancing crying babies on their hips, boys twirling coloured strings on their caps to attract attention or tapping with endless patience on the windows of idling cars, selling copies of Vogue, a grotesquely ironic choice of periodical to assign to a beggar. The country was a smashed mirror with some pieces reflecting the past, others the future. Between the tower blocks and tin-roofed slums a Dickensian tapestry was being endlessly unpicked and rewoven, a world where nothing could be achieved without carbon papers and rubber stamps, where ten did the work of one and one the work of ten.

Shere crunched the gears and pulled away from the men in some anger, swinging into the traffic without looking, so that trucks and rickshaws had to swerve from his path. 'So where do you want to go?' he asked, glancing at her in the mirror.

'I hadn't really—'

My relationship with this man has changed over the past week, she thought, holding onto the door strap. *He's so bored that he barely sees me. I thought I was in control, but now I wouldn't be able to do anything without him, and the further we get away from tourist spots, the more I am forced to rely on his services. The drivers run everything here.*

'Could you turn the air conditioning down for a while?' She flapped the guidebook at her breast.

He looked horrified by the idea, but did as she requested. She tried to study the book as they bounced through a convoy of trucks painted the shades of children's toys. Phrases swam up at her. 'Once known as the Land of Death'. 'Funeral pyres at dusk'. 'Nausea, cramps and exhaustion.' The pictures of the forts and palaces all looked the same; crenellated battlements, archways, turrets and domes. She turned the page. *Singh Pohl Monsoon Palace.* An ochre pavilion, perfectly proportioned, overgrown, surrounded by sandstone walkways and set on a perfectly square lake, the green water so still that it mirrored the building, doubling its size. She raised the book and pointed. 'I think I'd like to go here.'

He looked over his shoulder and studied the directions impassively. 'Forty-five kilometres, maybe more. It is not on our route.'

She read from the guidebook. *Vishnu, the most human of all gods, still haunts the forests around the Singh Pohl Palace. A flute, a peacock feather and the colour blue announce his presence. An earlier temple to the god Parjanya exists upon this site.*

'Yeah, that's where I want to go.' A decision had been made. She could sleep for a while. Ted never came with her on vacations. He said he wanted to travel, but the truth was that he hated leaving the US, and complained so much when he did that he destroyed any pleasure in the trip. Ted was never around these days.

Her mouth was dry. Shere had provided iced water and hand-towels for her, but she wanted something else. She had bought a bag of *pedas* and fruit candies studded with cardamom seeds in the market. They had the kind of sharply spiced flavours you would never find at home.

They passed a partially constructed motorway on which just two men were working, slowing raking gravel in a manner that spread it across each other's paths, each undoing the other's work. *How does anything run at all?* She wondered. *Over a billion people here, half of them shopkeepers selling nothing.*

Without the air conditioning she began to sweat. Her watch was gripping her wrist in a hot band, so she undid the clasp and dropped it in the bag at her feet. Pressing her head back into the rest, she studied the half-finished buildings of a small town slide by. Did no-one ever think to finish one house before starting another, or to plan the roads and pavements in such a way that prevented people from considering them interchangeable?

She liked the markets, the running and fetching, the tumble and bustle and sheer connectedness of everything. No-one seemed to be entirely alone, no matter how poor they were. Everyone had some kind of support system. At home she and Ted barricaded themselves in their gated community unlocked with an electronic key fob, and only saw the neighbours departing or arriving at holiday seasons. *If I needed help and couldn't get to the phone, I'd have to lie there until Ted got home,* she thought, *even assuming he was in town.*

The car screeched to a stop. In the road ahead, two half-starved dogs were fighting. One had buried its teeth in the other's left haunch. Loops of blood and spittle flecked the sidewalk as they rolled over each other. She opened the window an inch and the oppressive heat leaked in. Shere could not understand why his passenger was refusing the comfort of refrigerated air. *This place disgusts and frightens me,* she thought, *and yet I am drawn in. It makes me dream again.*

27

She was touring with three large pieces of Louis Vitton luggage. The driver did not seem to think this unusual. He was probably used to the strange habits of westerners, who toured as though they were moving house. Shere knew a place where they could stop for something to eat. A wall of oven-heat touched her as she stepped stiffly from the car. Ahead was a low white block in a bare, dusty yard. The straight road passed it, but there was nothing to see in either direction.

An ancient fiddle player witnessed her arrival, stood up and began to play a painful dirge until she had passed. The restaurant looked shut, but Shere waved her ahead.

'You don't want to come eat with me?' she asked.

'I have my own lunch.' Shere smiled and wobbled his head in apology. As she approached the restaurant doors she saw the lights flicker on in the dark interior. Waiters were scurrying to don their white coats. She ate Butter Chicken and Pashwari Nan alone beside a window with cracked panes of plastic that had been stuffed with toilet paper to keep out the dust. The food was sensational, the bathroom after, horrific. She sat in the car with a gurgling stomach as the roads grew dustier, browner, emptier. On the horizon, a line of wooded hills appeared. Finally, the road curved and climbed. It grew hotter and closer, until she felt as if she was suffocating.

'The rains are coming,' he said, reading her thoughts, 'maybe tonight.'

'How much further?' she asked, but received no reply. *I shouldn't have picked this place,* she admonished herself, *too far away, and even the driver doesn't seem to be sure of its whereabouts.*

They reached a string of small villages where everything glistened with marble dust. Outside every house and shop stood large carved statues of Hindu gods. Men sat cross-legged on their forecourts, chipping away at great white blocks from which the gods were slowly breaking free. She could differentiate some now; Ganesha, Hanuman, Brahma, Shakti and Shiva, but the rest still looked the same. A guide had told her that there were over 330,000 to choose from. Who on earth bought these huge statues? They stood in rows like sentries on guard duty, ignored by children who probably found them as familiar as relatives.

A low brick wall—half finished, of course—ran around the edge of the town. She caught a glimpse of a sandstone building between the trees. 'I think the palace is over there,' said Shere. 'My friend tells me the World Heritage people, they came to look, and were going to make it a site of special significance. Good for tourism. But they decided not to.'

'Why?'

'Politics. I don't know.'

'Any tourists here now?'

'No, none. Not since the bombings. This is a ghost palace. Nobody comes here at night. Only the spirits live here now. You will want to walk in the palace?'

'Yes, I think so.'

'There is no guide for you.'

Good, she thought, *I've had enough of standing in the heat listening to earnest men reeling off building statistics.* 'Do you have any more cold water I can take with me?'

'We can stop.' He pulled up beside a small shop and purchased a bottle of water for her. While she waited in the car, a handful of children ran to the window and started tapping on the glass with distracted insistence. When she'd first arrived in the country, she had given all her small change to these hollow-eyed creatures, but the driver had stopped her, explaining that they were forced to pay their earnings back to gang-runners in the slums. After a few days she realised that her generosity could change nothing and would do nobody good in the long run.

Shere returned and they drove toward the palace. He swung the car off the main highway onto a back road, between tall dusty trees whose branches bent into arches from the weight of their own high leaves. A flock of green parrots blasted screeching into the air above them. Then there was only heat and silence.

She looked for a sign or a ticket booth, but there was nothing to mark the entrance to the palace. A single kitchen chair stood by a gap in the wall, where a guard usually sat. Drawn by the sound of the car, a few tiny children appeared, scampering toward her as they drew to a stop. Shere turned off the engine, then took a call on his mobile.

One small boy remained against the wall, holding back from the group. He watched Marion with the kind of sad resignation one usually only saw in disappointed old men. When the boy realised that he had gained her attention, he pushed away from the wall and bunched his fingertips, gesturing to his mouth. Ignoring the others, she beckoned him over.

Her belongings were grouped around her on the back seat. She found the brown paper bag of candies and waited. His shyness surprised her. He seemed to be waiting for some kind of a sign. She realised she was frowning, and smiled instead.

He came a little nearer, then stopped. She held the sweets up against the window, remaining motionless. The other children saw that she was not looking at them, and gradually dispersed. *I choose you,* she thought, *because you are trying hard not to look as if you care.*

Shere finished his phone call and turned to see what was happening.

The boy remained with his hands by his sides, studying her, as if trying to see a friendly spirit within. He cautiously approached, but two little girls remained at the window with their hands outstretched, blocking his way.

Marion handed them each a silver-wrapped sweet, then passed the bag through the window to the boy. Clutching it to his chest, his serious eyes briefly locked with hers, and he ran away. She watched him go with a vague sense of dissatisfaction. *What did you expect, that he would show gratitude?*

'You are ready to visit?'

'I'm ready,' she sighed, feeling suddenly empty. 'You don't have to come with me, I can find it.'

'I can come with you.' He didn't sound keen.

'It's fine, I have this. It's all I need.' She held up the guide and tapped the cover, then slipped out of the car.

'I'll be here.' Shere got out, opened her door, then took the opportunity to light a cigarette.

'I know you will. I won't be long.'

Slipping the guide into her back pocket, she followed the overgrown path into the complex. Ahead, a family of white-haired monkeys with triangular black faces scattered at her approach. *Everyone's a part of something here,* she thought, *even the monkeys. I'd like to be part of something. Would Ted even notice if I didn't come back?* The incline to the palace was low but steady, and the heat was dense, tangible. Sweat formed on her face, in the small of her back. *Something must break soon,* she thought, *this is unbearable.*

The first building she reached was a pillared pavilion containing a bull shrine. The carved black bull was life-sized and kneeling, garlanded with artificial jasmine flowers, so perhaps the villagers were still worshipping here. Beyond this, though, came disappointment. The lake had dried out, and appeared as a

31

shallow rubble-strewn cavity in the ground, littered with plastic bottles. *Due to global warming,* she had read, *the shrinking monsoon season means that lakes and rivers all over India are drying up, many to vanish forever.*

The shattered remains of a pair of marble lions guarded the arched entrance to a platformed complex, and a tall Mughal swing had been placed by rooms that she knew would have once have housed a harem. But the swing itself had fallen into disrepair, and the semi-precious gems that should have been inset in the arch had long ago been prised out by robbers. The main pavilion was complete, but in a sorry state. Instead of the smooth amber and ochre walls in the photographs, she found herself looking at colours that had faded and died to streaked greys and dirty browns. The inset mirrors and plaster carvings of the interior walls were ruined, and the ornate *jaali* screens were nowhere to be seen. Nothing was as it appeared in the guidebook. *Next time buy a recent edition,* she reminded herself. *Like there'll be a next time. Ted wouldn't allow it again.*

Set at right-angles to the pavilion was a structure raised on four great fluted plinths, each beset by a pair of squat lotus urns, but the building did not look safe enough to enter. In the quadrangle formed by the buildings, bathing tanks and a complex network of stone gullies must once have been filled with water, but were now dried out and dead. She cupped her hands to shield out the sunlight, and looked to the roof, which was lined with terracotta pitchers. Somewhere in the woods beyond, a bird thrashed and screamed.

There were other buildings to explore, a small mosque with dried-out marigold garlands on its steps, a partially ruined tomb, but she did not have the energy to investigate them all. Outside the royal apartments, peacocks pecked at the sunbleached ground. Clearly the villagers had been here, for the birds' tail-feathers had been plucked, presumably to sell at the market.

In the shadows of the tomb's canopy she saw a small seated figure, and immediately recognised the boy. *He's different to the others,* she thought, *quiet and more thoughtful.* Through the trees she could make out the far edge of the village. After studying the scene for a few more moments, she turned to make her way back. *If I had seen this ten days ago I'd have been more impressed, but I've walked through too many of them now. They're all the same. They lack life.*

She tore open a moist tissue and wiped her forehead. She found Shere leaning beside the car, smoking. Surprised by her fast return, he went to grind out the cigarette. 'It's okay,' she told him, 'take your time.'

She opened the passenger door and slid onto the back seat. The sun was still high. They had stopped early for lunch. Surely it could only be about two o'clock. She fished on the floor for the sweet bag containing her watch, then remembered that she had given the bag to the boy.

How could she have been so stupid? What had she been thinking? The watch had been a gift from Ted, solemnly presented in order to make amends for his behaviour. The damned thing was encrusted with diamonds and worth around fourteen thousand dollars, even now. She had never really liked it, but that was less to do with its appearance and more because it represented an expensive apology. Over the years she had grown so blasé about wearing it that she had become careless.

The boy had been sitting in one of the temples in the palace. She had to go back and find him.

Shere caught her alarm. 'Where are you going?'

'My watch. The boy.' It was not an explanation, but all that she could manage right now. The monkeys scattered as she strode back up the path thinking *Insurance, sales receipt, Ted, how will he ever be persuaded to give it back—*

As she approached the palace's large central pavilion, she became aware of the change in light all around her. The gardens had lost the little colour they possessed, darkening to olive, the walls deepening to camelskin.

She crossed a cracked courtyard and climbed the palace platforms, peering through the stone latticework in search of the child. She had her purse; she would offer him rupees and have him return the watch. After all, what would he want with such a thing?

She became aware of a presence behind her, a tall figure bisected by shadows. She turned, startled, and found herself facing a huge stone statue of a god wearing a strange cloud-crown. He was holding an eight-petalled plant in each hand. On the floor was a wooden plaque written in English. It read;

> PARJANYA is the Old God of The Heavens. He rules lightning, thunder and rain. He controls the procreation of plants and animals, but can also punish sinners. His powers are a mighty wonder to behold.

She studied his wind-damaged face. A faint but defiant smile played on his lips, as if he wished to play a game, or be challenged. As if he was waiting to show his strength. She shivered. A wind had risen. Dry leaves scuttled across the terrazzo floor. In the last few minutes a wall of rolling cloud had appeared on the horizon and was sliding across the sky like a steel shutter.

Stepping back from the statue, which seemed to be smiling at her in the half-light, she headed from one building to the next until she reached the sunken groves of the *charbargh*, the walled paradise garden divided in four quarters to represent the four parts of life, but the boy was nowhere to be found.

34

Mistake at the Monsoon Palace

The only thing she could do now was persuade Shere to take her to the village and ask the shopkeepers if they had seen him, but already she sensed that they would unite behind the child and her mission would fail.

The first fat drop stained the dust at her feet like ink falling from a pen nib. It made an audible *ploc* as it landed. A second, *tac*, hit the steps. Looking up, she saw that the clouds entirely covered the sky. Moments later the droplets multiplied by tens, hundreds, thousands, millions, from a shower to a roaring downpour, to a thunderous cascade, to a sound like the end of the world. Visibility dropped to zero and she stumbled up the steps into the open-sided pavilion, watching in wonder as rain unlike any she had ever seen deluged the palace.

At his car, Shere swore and threw down his cigarette as the first drops fell. He heard raised voices; a massive cheer of excitement filtered through the trees from the village. His client would already be soaked unless she had managed to take shelter. If she complained to the tour company, they would dock his pay or worse, place him on a circuit where he could make no money from the shops and restaurants he recommended.

There was no point in looking for her; the uphill path was already turning into a mudslide. She would have to wait for a break and return as best she could.

A change was sweeping over the monsoon palace. The dried out walls had blossomed into bright ambers, ochres and fiery reds. Tiles were washed of their dust to reveal a fierce blue glaze beneath. Mosaic panels covered with geometric lapis motifs sprouted and bloomed like orchids, glistening ornamental patterns emerging on the *chhatris* of the pavilions. Grey walls revealed hidden blues, yellows and greens. Earth was washed from the courtyard to reveal a polished marble floor inlaid with designs; floral bouquets, fruit trees and wine decanters. The gutters filled with rivulets that became gurgling streams, then pounding torrents, water shooting out of stonework spouts as the fountains sputtered into life. Marion grabbed the wet pages of the guidebook and searched for the pictures of the palace.

But it is the magic of the monsoon that restores the Palace, she read, *for this forgotten complex of sandstone buildings and gardens was created to activate special effects during the rainy season that would delight the Bharatpur kings. The palace's reservoirs are designed to fill instantly, fed by water-steps which pump streams through pipes to the peacock fountains.*

Following the guide's floor plan, she looked straight ahead and saw that what she had mistaken for piles of pale stones were in fact great marble peacocks. Rain was rushing down the steep gullies to be forced into the narrow stone pipes surrounding the birds. Water gushed from behind their long necks in shimmering rainbow fans, perfectly replicating the bird's plumage. Marion was stunned. All about her, pipes and pillars were spouting water shapes, birds, animals, flowers. The pavilion's overhanging balconies and kiosks channelled rain into intricate patterns that held formation for a moment before breaking apart and falling to earth.

The palace had been built to provide royal delight during the monsoon. It needed heavy rain to come alive. Water swelled and saturated the parched earth and the arched halls around her, filling them with colour and vigour. She walked, then ran through the white cascades between the inundated pools and reservoirs.

A long low belch of thunder sounded from somewhere between the ground and the clouds. Looking to the roof of the opposite pavilion, she saw a series of heavy lithic balls forced by sprays and jets of water to roll slowly across the concave roof, then back from the far side, artificially producing the sounds of a storm. The ditches around her were filling fast. Shielded from the downpour, they formed graceful mirror geometries that reflected the falling rain. She looked to where she had last seen the boy sitting. The curiously curved roof of the tomb now made sense; its upturned reflection was that of a boat, ferrying its precious cargo to safety.

She was crying uncontrollably now, tears pouring down her cheeks in an unstoppable flow. Her white shirt was stuck to her shoulders, her breasts. She fought the urge to tear the transparent material from her body and wade into the lake. A sense of understanding flooded through her, filling her with compassion. She no longer cared about her watch, her luggage, her husband, her home. The trappings of her life had vanished in the revelation of the tempest. Unashamed of crying or calling to the gods, her voice joined the thousands of others who celebrated the coming of the monsoon.

The boy splashed through the streets with the paper bag clutched in his fist, and found his uncle closing because of the rains. Uncle Javed's decision to delay the repairs to his roof would cost him dearly. Later on this very night, part of the shop's ceiling would fall in and ruin his new stock of winter jackets and saris.

The boy showed his uncle the watch, and received a clip across the ear for his trouble. 'Oh Karan, you will cause your mother to die of despair,' he scolded, 'for producing another little thief like your brother. Hasn't the poor woman had enough trouble in her miserable life? Why do you want to see her suffer further?'

'I didn't steal it,' Karan insisted. 'A rich American lady opened the window of her car and handed it to me.'

'Such a little liar!' Uncle Javed cried, trying to seize the boy's thin neck. 'What kind of monster have we raised that he should steal from the very people who come here in trust? Was she very rich?'

'You steal from them all the time,' said Karan, stepping back from his uncle's grabbing hands, 'every time you sell them a shawl and tell them it was sewn by a lady who took twenty months to make it all by hand.'

'That is the art of business, you rude child. Every woman wants to be told the story behind her purchase, in order to make it more of a bargain.'

'But your stories aren't true.'

'They are exactly what people wish to believe. Price has nothing to do with value. And this—' he held the glittering watch aloft, '—must go back to the tourist you stole it from.'

'But I'm sure she has gone.'

'Did you look for her?'

'No.'

'Well, that is a blessing. My heart aches to think of the trouble you would have caused by making her think you were a thief. Come on, we have to visit old Mister Chauhan. He will be able to tell us how much the watch is worth. We must know how big a thief you have become, in order to find the right penance for your sin.'

Karan reluctantly agreed to go along, but first he made sure that Uncle Javed returned the bag to him.

The boys in the village said that Mister Chauhan was about five hundred years old, and had once been introduced to Queen Victoria in Old Bombay. His skin was so wrinkled, it looked to Karan as if someone had magically transferred his features to a brown paper bag, then screwed the bag up and flattened it out imperfectly. Mister Chauhan owned a brass-rimmed magnifying glass the size of a hotel dinner plate. He raised it by a pair of horn handles and held it over the watch on his cluttered desk. For several minutes there was complete silence in the cramped antique shop. Finally he set down the glass and turned to the boy.

'There are thirty-six diamonds of extremely high quality inside this watch-casing, but there is also something missing.'

'Missing?' Uncle Javed looked at his nephew in puzzlement.

'No serial number,' said Mister Chauhan. 'On Cartier watches of this type there are two types of authentication. On the downward stroke of the Roman numeral seven one can see, with the aid of a strong magnifier, the word 'Cartier' written in script. That is one sign. The other is the serial number on the back of the casing, but there is none.'

'So typical that my thieving nephew should choose to steal a worthless fake,' Uncle Javed complained, giving the boy another clip around the ear.

'I did not say it was a fake,' Mister Chauhan continued. 'This watch is very genuine indeed. It is extremely rare, so rare that someone has erased the number to prevent it from being traced. Every Cartier can be traced by its number.'

'Why would somebody remove it?' asked Uncle Javed.

Uncle Chauhan sucked his teeth and thought for a moment. "I can think of two very good reasons. Either the person who bought it did not wish it to be found, because he made the purchase with bad money.'

'He avoids his taxes. He is a crook.'

'Something like that.'

'What is the other reason?'

'A man might make such a purchase for his mistress, whose name he does not wish to be recorded on papers as the watch's owner.'

'The lady was not a mistress,' said Karan, 'she was a wife.'

'Then perhaps her husband repents and gives the watch he buys his mistress to his wife, after first taking the precautionary measure of removing the serial number.'

Uncle Javed looked as if he had just seen a fortune fly out of the window.

'Mister Chauhan, you make a fine storyteller,' laughed Karan. 'If I did not know you better, I might be tempted to think that you were inventing such a marvellous story so that I might agree to sell it for a small amount.'

'The watch cannot be repaired or serviced by Cartier,' Mister Chauhan explained. 'And this is the very thing that any prospective buyer would want.'

But even as he looked into the boy's unblinking brown eyes, Mister Chauhan knew he had lost. For this was India, where the past was not important, and anything could be repaired. He sighed and ordered the *chai* to be brewed, knowing that it would be a long evening. The bargaining began in earnest. Karan had seen the greedy fire in Mister Chauhan's eyes, and knew that the process of negotiation would be lengthy and arduous.

In fact, the formalities took three days and involved one boy and five men from two villages. Part of the problem was that the arrangement had to be kept away from the knowledge of the local police constabulary in order to avoid an unacceptable level of commission being deducted from the sale. At the conclusion of the deal much money was assembled, assurances were written out, whisky and *masala* tea was poured, everyone involved was sworn to silence, and Karan rode the train to Bangalore, to begin a new life.

Mistake at the Monsoon Palace

Shere Banjara, the driver for Jacaranda Tours, fifty two years old and married with five children, was severely reprimanded and fined for the loss of his charge. The paperwork involved took over a year to sort out. Finally he was moved from his base in Delhi to Kolkotta, where he quickly learned that the new circuit could reap him unexpected rewards from a fresh generation of middle-class businessmen looking to buy carpets and tapestries for their second homes.

As the years passed, the dry and rainy seasons replaced each other like cards falling upon a gaming table. The monsoon palace was denied World Heritage status due to a dispute over the ownership of its land, and remained overgrown and forgotten by all except the monkeys, doves and peacocks, who lived within its evening shadows. Parjanya sat in the dusty shadows and bided his time.

Then, one overheated day, just before the arrival of the monsoon, when the air was so scorched that it felt like you might carve a hole in it to breathe, some workers angrily threw their pickaxes and shovels down onto the hard dry soil and started shouting at one another.

'What the bloody hell is going on here?' asked the project foreman, striding over. Work had fallen behind, and it was starting to look as if they would not be finished before the rains came, which would be disastrous because the road had not yet been sealed and they needed to take the shack down now.

'The villagers tell us we cannot remove Maran or we will bring bad luck to the area,' said one of the workmen. 'We need to dismantle any obstacle today.'

'Wait, you are talking about this? *This?*' The foreman pointed to the chaotic arrangement of tin huts that stood in their path and began to laugh. 'Bulldoze it flat. Pass me a pickaxe and I'll do it myself.' He spat *paan* on the ground dismissively.

'You don't understand. A promise was made that Maran would never be moved.'

'Who was this promise made to?'

'An old man called Javed who lived in the village.'

'Javed? That scoundrel? He has been dead for over five years! The past is the past. Knock it down.'

The workmen reluctantly moved toward their tools, but before they could continue their work, a horn sounded and they were forced to move to the sides of the road to allow for the arrival of a white Mercedes. Everyone agreed that the man who emerged from the rear seat looked like a younger version of Shahrukh Kahn, the Bollywood superstar. He walked over to the tin huts, examined them and beckoned the foreman.

'How far over the boundary line?'

The foreman looked at the ground and thought. 'Twenty feet, at least.'

'You know how long Maran has lived here?'

'The men tell me fifteen years.'

'Sixteen. You know why?'

'Something to do with guarding the palace and keeping it in good repair, but there's no paperwork—'

'You don't need paperwork for everything. Let me deal with this.' As he approached the huts, a pair of green parrots screamed and rocked the ornate wire cage that hung from the lintel above the front door. He tapped respectfully and stepped back, waiting.

The grey-haired woman who appeared in the doorway studied her visitor and smiled. 'Come inside,' she instructed. 'I wasn't sure if you would get here in time. The *chai* is almost ready. I've learned to like it sweet. I never took sugar at home. Have that chair in the corner, but be careful, the leg is broken.'

Mistake at the Monsoon Palace

The interior of the hut was crowded with decorative ornaments that had been presented to her by the villagers over the years, mostly Hindu gods. 'Let me look at you.'

Karan adjusted his collar and slicked back his hair, ready for inspection. 'I did not believe you would stay, Maran.'

'Marion,' she corrected. 'Oh, I come from a long line of very determined women. Besides, if I deserted my palace, who else would do the job? You people are losing respect for your past, all this rushing toward the future.'

'And "you people" have not done the same?' asked Karan. 'This is not your palace. It is not a cause you can simply adopt, like a child.'

In the soft light Marion looked younger than her years, the way she had been when he first saw her. 'You're right, of course. I can't explain what I feel. But I know you can't take his land.' She touched her bare tanned neck, remembering. 'I wanted to look nice for you but the damned monkey took my necklace. He's probably buried it out by the *jharna*.'

'The gardens of the monsoon palace have never been accurately measured, you know. We could go beyond their walls right now, trim a hundred yards off and no-one would ever know.'

'Shame on you, to even think of such a thing. He will know. Parjanya will know.'

'I have no other choice. But you, do you really want to stay on here?'

'I have no other choice either. I burned my bridges long ago.'

'Where is your husband?'

'Maybe he stayed with his mistress,' she said carelessly. 'I wrote him some letters. I don't know if he got them.'

'I'm sorry.'

43

'Don't be, I'm not. I'll become like the old British ladies who still live on in Delhi, complaining about their landlords and going slowly crazy. Something about this place encourages the irrational. . . .'

'I could move you back into the village. Javed's children have offered you a home.'

'No,' she said firmly, 'I need to be within sight of the pavilion. I've seen the designs for your little housing project, Karan. A gated community? I stayed here to get away from such things. Don't tell me it's progress, because it's nothing of the kind.'

'It's what people want.' Karan smiled. 'Didn't you know, we're all middle class now, even if our castes can never change.'

'Well, it seems to me that we have to strike a deal, but I have no cards to play. Are you hungry? I could make you some *paneer*.'

'No, I had a pizza.'

'You could have me thrown off the site tonight, if that's what you want.'

'I could, but you know I would never do it.' He sipped his *masala*. 'You make this better than my mother used to. So, this is what we'll do. You stay here. I'll shift the boundary back, everyone's happy.'

'Everyone except Parjanya.'

'It is the only solution I can offer.'

'It sounds like you already had that in mind. You can't do it without changing the planning application, can you?'

'I can change the application with a few handfuls of rupees. We need to reduce the size of the estate because the surveyors are arriving from Delhi next week.'

'It's a shame. I thought the monsoon palace would eventually be accepted as a World Heritage site. Now, more than ever,

Parjanya needs a guardian here.' Marion laughed softly to herself.

'What is funny?' Karan asked.

'I was foolish enough to think that such an ancient, magnificent monument might be saved by a bag of sweets,' she replied.

'The palace will be protected, but the condition is the partial surrender of its grounds,' said Karan.

'He will not let you take his land,' she said simply.

'Listen, Marion, I have respect for you, but you cannot change what must be done.' Enough. She exasperated him. Karan rose and took his leave. Outside, as he spoke to his foreman, she imagined the desiccated ground receiving fat drops of quenching rain.

The men moved in. The yellow bulldozers and earthmovers backed away from the hut, but surged toward the low dry-stone walls and pushed straight through them, gouging channels in the soft red earth. The workmen marched forward behind the vehicles, an advancing army clad in bright protective jackets.

Marion stood in the doorway and watched, smiling to herself.

They cannot steal the land you have protected for me, Parjanya hissed in her ear. *They are arrogant enough to think that their machines will make a difference, but they forget I control the Heavens.*

Parjanya made the rains come. She looked up into the sky and saw it cloud over within a few seconds. The first bolt of lightning split the air and hit the cabin of the lead earthmover. A scream came from within. Men swarmed around the stalled vehicle as smoke billowed from its electrics.

It was the heaviest monsoon squall she had ever witnessed. The rain increased until nothing could be discerned from the door of the hut. She heard the ominous rumble of wet earth as a

45

torrent of mud poured over the broken walls, punching the workmen's legs from under them, swallowing them in thick brown effluvium. The men were all choked and drowned, or were crushed and buried. Their machines were overturned on top of them, hammering them flat, bursting their soft shells into the bubbling cauldron of mud. The monkeys stared out from the shelter of the palace, hooting in triumph. Soon the mud would dry again and it would be as if the workmen were never here.

A beatific smile crept over Marion's face as she returned to make fresh tea.

Karan unknotted his tie and fanned himself in the blast-furnace heat. He watched Marion slowly retreat into the shadows, lost inside her visions. One of the workmen jammed his shovel into the hard dry earth, leaned back and caught his eye, grinning knowingly. *Pāgala aurata.* Crazy lady.

Karan wondered what was going through Marion's head. It was a funny thing about those who came to stay; the ones who didn't believe often ended up believing a little too much.

Let her keep her dreams, he thought. *I'll only take eighty yards from the garden. No-one will notice. If they ask, I'll tell them it was a mistake.*

Somewhere in the dense treetops behind him, the first cool breezes rose.

THE SWINGER
Rhys Hughes

There was a haunted tree in the garden of the hotel. Everyone knew it was a haunted tree, though they treated it as a joke or a mascot, something that didn't need to be taken seriously. Only Uncle Dylan had authentic respect for the old tales, the gnarled legends.

It was the highest cedar among a dozen others and a curiously straight branch jabbed out near the very top, like the crossbeam of a gallows. The stories insisted that no bird dared perch there; but I saw several ravens in a line on it once, and I waved at them.

One of my habits, waving at birds, an energy-efficient royal wave that must look absurd to anyone else. I have been doing it since I was a child, secretly, with much embarrassment, like those people who salute magpies by pretending to scratch their foreheads.

This tree was part of my soul and my dreams.

But I never looked at it properly.

It was with amazement that I realised that the reason why it was higher than its neighbours was because it stood on the summit of a grassy mound, a bizarrely symmetrical cone of densely packed soil. The tree was actually fairly short, compacted, stunted.

Uncle Dylan had hung lanterns in the limbs of the other cedars, paper spheres with little candles inside, so that they resembled gigantic oranges that had suddenly appeared where they shouldn't; but the haunted tree he left undecorated in the evenings, a stark silhouette against the starry sky. I didn't believe he had no spare lanterns.

'It's for the sake of the guests,' he told me once.

'I'm not fooled by that,' I said.

He sighed and shrugged, then turned to wipe clean the beer glasses. A fire of logs snapped and hissed in the grate; the click of cribbage pegs and the plucking of a harp; the creak of the rusty sign outside. These made the music of the place, a false re-enactment of a time that never truly existed, the merry days of yore, of pastoral life.

Uncle Dylan was obsessed with his personal vision of what the ancient times must have been like. In vain I objected to his notions and explained in detail the brutality endured by our remote ancestors. The good yeomen waded in filth; they crouched in squalor; for the most part, they beat each other with sticks. But he wouldn't listen.

Matthew Loveday, a writer and historian, shared similar utopian ideals and mindlessly approved every one of Uncle Dylan's prejudices, agreeing that the hotel had stood on the spot for eight hundred years at least, that a monastery had existed here before it, that primitive men had danced to an unknown god thousands of years earlier around standing stones that must have been carted away by a greedy king.

Like most of our long-term guests, Loveday was from England and he had come here to sample a past long since covered by concrete in his own land. Uncle Dylan lived up to his expectations perfectly, even playing the old raconteur with greater than usual relish, lighting a pipe stuffed with a foul and oily smuggled tobacco and saying:

'Oh yes! we have a ghost. A man of letters like yourself. I found him swinging one morning under the tree, dangling on the end of a long rope from the highest branch. And now his spirit wanders the garden wailing. A miserable sod. Does he rattle things? He ransacked the kitchen, looking for a knife with which to cut himself down.'

'And did he find one?' Loveday asked, gazing through the window at the haunted tree with a pensive expression.

'No,' said Uncle Dylan, abruptly and with a scowl.

'So his ghost is unsatisfied?'

'Yes, yes! And they say he seeks one like himself to give him aid; but I don't know who "they" are to say such things, so I can't be certain and I can't even ask them to hold their tongues.'

'Why should anyone wish to hold their tongue?'

Uncle Dylan thrust out his own pink organ from between his thick lips and clutched it in both hands; that's how large a tongue he had. For a full minute he held it, then let it go and it slithered back into his mouth like a chastised flatworm, and Uncle Dylan's throat pulsated as if it wanted to slide down even deeper than was normal.

'It's not an unpleasant thing to do, that's why.'

'I don't suppose it is,' said Loveday.

I smiled into my beer. The wind whistled around the house. Indeed it was getting quite eerie again. The fire in the hearth was dying; the embers glowed faintly in a gale howling down the chimney. As the mischievous Uncle Dylan spouted more of his nonsense, and as Loveday leaned closer to hear it, I couldn't resist an interruption.

'It won't last,' I said. 'They're all coming down, every last one of the cedars. The entire garden will be concreted over. Then a car park, electric lighting and satellite television aerial. . . .'

Uncle Dylan scowled. It had taken me a year to persuade him that the hotel would be better off without the overgrown wilderness of a garden. Ecologically minded, he had objected to the felling of trees on principle, but yielded after I made him aware of a few facts concerning increased profits. The haunted tree he wanted to be made exempt, of course. Finally, I'd persuaded him that it would look so ungainly standing atop its mound all by itself, that we really had no choice.

'Times do change,' he admitted to himself. Loveday, however, didn't seem at all disconcerted by this threat to his beloved past, this end of a heritage right under his very nose. He was in high good humour. His latest novel, he explained, had just been published. It was, he felt sure, his masterpiece, an effort that would finally secure his place in the pantheon of great moderns. He drained his glass.

'Let's drink to my success and to the next one!'

He bought a round for the three of us. I felt uncomfortable sipping the ale of a man I eagerly wanted to disillusion, to drown in disappointment, to send back to England, his tales between his legs. I can't explain why I felt this aversion to the man. An instinct.

'There's a legend about the man who hung himself,' Uncle Dylan said in a very small voice and I blinked at him.

'Do you have to? I've heard them all many times.'

'Not this one, you haven't.'

'What do you mean?' in my sharpest tone.

'I've kept it to myself all these years. I *am* allowed to have secrets that you don't. There's no law against that.'

'Well, tell us the legend!' gasped Loveday.

He was desperate to know more, to gather every fact, every fiction and speck of rumour, every flake of hearsay about the case. Why it fascinated him so intensely, I couldn't understand.

'It is said that if a man manages to hang himself in that garden *higher* than the top of the haunted tree, he'll earn the right to live in any period of history he desires. Myself, I would go right back to the Middle Ages, to the time of Llewellyn the Great; but though I believe the legend, I just can't think of a way of fulfilling its terms.'

Loveday was impressed by this. He drank his beer in slow gulps like a man drinking his own excellent destiny.

'Time travel through hanging,' he said at last.

Uncle Dylan nodded. 'Apparently.'

'How can this be possible? You are talking nonsense!' I interjected, a false but enormous grin on my face. 'The man killed himself two decades ago; he's not a legend yet, not a tradition.'

Uncle Dylan swivelled his head like an owl, his eyes unmoving, facing me with an infinite weariness, and sighed. 'Yes, the legend of the hanged man predates the reality of the event. Why should that be impossible? It's an assumption that a legend follows the truth; it's a distortion of the facts. After all, it's time travel we are debating.'

'We're not *debating* anything,' I snarled bitterly.

Loveday turned once again to stare through the window at the tree and the mound. He spoke without caring whether we heard or not. 'The story is ridiculous, no doubt about it, but that's no argument against it. In fact it has a ring of truth about it on some level.'

A harp player on a nearby table struck a soft chord.

'You are mad, both of you,' I said.

Uncle Dylan nodded. 'Absolutely. But so are you.'

My mood lightened. I laughed and stood and bade them goodnight. It was early but I had a headache and stiff neck. Better to leave them to their strange games and hobbies, the defective worship of a past glued together from memories of films and novels, where archers in green trousers shot arrows at juggled apples and damsels wore hats as tall as towers, ribbons streaming from them like levitating rivers.

51

Dark World

ℵ

I lay on my hard bed, my skeleton shifting inside me, the storm outside getting worse and creaking anything it could, including the teeth of the howling dog in the rain somewhere who bit the wind valiantly, foolishly, annoyingly until midnight clanged on the church clock in the village, the dull notes whipped away, carried off like pewter plates by hungry pirates, for the coast was once infested with them.

Sleep eluded me and I felt almost suffocated or crushed by the weight of the cliché I seemed to have become embedded in; the stormy night, a feeling of helplessness in the face of forces supernatural, malign, perhaps, or just impossible, which is almost as bad.

But at last I had to admit defeat and get up, dress myself and stand at the tiny warped window of my attic room.

And then came the flash of lightning that confirmed my suspicions I wasn't a real man but an actor in a drama, a cheaply produced horror play or film; for the tree seemed flat, a cardboard cut-out, in the instantaneous glare of the electric discharge; and from the highest branch swung a man, the puppet I knew to be Matthew Loveday.

I remained calmer than perhaps I should have. I stood for a full minute and peered into the darkness, waiting for the next flash before I went into action. I don't understand this delay; I think it was just bafflement or even a strange sort of boredom. Then the thunder boomed and knocked me out of my complacency like a sonic elbow in the ribs. I flinched, turned and ran down the stairs to the hotel's rear door.

The next flash, even brighter and more intense, came while I was still on the stairwell. I smelled it and felt my hairs prickle. I heard heavy feet somewhere, one of the guests or else a strange acoustic trick. Probably not Uncle Dylan, who was such a deep sleeper he was difficult to rouse even at times of emergency. Once, when a lorry crashed into the lobby of the hotel in the early hours after the driver fell asleep at the wheel, Uncle Dylan remained blissfully lost in dreams.

I reached the bottom of the stairs, twisted the door handle and felt the punch of the wind on my creased brow. I had to physically lean forward at an absurd angle in order to push myself across the threshold into the garden. The door slammed behind me so loudly that it came off its hinges and clattered to the floor in time with the next roll of thunder. The body was kicking; it wasn't too late to save him.

'Loveday, you fool! What sort of game is this?' I cried.

My useless words of chastisement, a sop to my own feelings of guilt at not hurrying faster to his assistance, were shredded by the wind, mangled into disconnected sounds, grunts and clicks.

I raced across the sodden lawn to the haunted tree. The long grass was undulating, lapping at my legs as I plunged forward. I was aware that the tree was a likely target for a lightning strike, being the tallest object in the vicinity, but I felt no concern about that.

My desire seemed simply to reach the legs of the dying man, to touch his feet, to console him with my presence. There was no way I could cut him down, for I had forgotten to bring a knife. But I didn't return to the hotel to fetch one. My quest was spiritual.

That sounds ludicrous, callous, deluded, and doubtless my response to this tragedy was all three. But I'm not justifying myself, merely reporting my actions. I felt drunk, not wholly sane; but a part of my mind retained a lucidity that sneered at the rest of me, at my impetuous dash across damp electric tingling shadows to stand under the shoes of a suicide. Already he was kicking with less force, twitching less.

I stumbled to a halt near him. He had used a very long rope and he was lucky that the drop hadn't decapitated him. Perhaps he had somehow let himself down gradually. His feet were six feet above the lawn; to one side stood the mound and the tree reared up from the rounded apex of that, so he was suspended at a lower point than the base of the trunk. I found this a fascinating paradox; a man who had hung himself successfully at a level lower than the tree itself. I stood and shook.

Water streamed over my face. Another flash of lightning made crazy shadows of twisted branches and leaves. Then the shadow of the rope no longer hung straight but began gently oscillating from side to side. Weird how I noticed this from the shadow before learning it from the rope itself, almost as if I couldn't bear to regard as real the scene before me; I had to have it filtered through its own silhouettes.

Like a pendulum gathering momentum, the dying body of Loveday on the end of its vicious tether was pushed by the wind in a growing arc. The whoosh of its passage through the air was audible despite the aftershocks of thunder that echoed in the labyrinths of my ears. I retreated a step, as if a blade swung there in place of a flesh body.

'This is a travesty. Please stop!' I howled at nobody.

But I was rightly ignored, not merely by Loveday, but circumstances also. The tree, the storm, the night, the thick atmosphere of viciousness, my own fear in my own bones, everything.

The invisible hands of an adult wind imparted energy to this man, who was a sullen dying child, with as much efficiency as if he was perched on a playground swing and had to be set in motion by an outside force before he could utilise his legs to keep going, to make the arc wider by swinging his heavy limbs back and forth rhythmically.

As the rope tightened to take the strain it began to sing a note, to drone an accompaniment to the thunder's occasional timpani. On stage with this minimal percussive orchestra of nightmare, I watched the metronome that had once been a writer swing wider and wider, his tempo increasing as an unnatural harmony was established between the gusts and his kicking legs that served to propel him continually faster.

I fought a desire to fling myself forward onto him, to clutch at his legs, less to slow him down than to be taken away, to experience the wildness of the ride, to replay with perverted nostalgia the bravest adventures of a childhood spent swinging from trees on ropes.

The pendulum gathered energy, the pitch of the stretched note rasped higher and the branch sagged but did not snap.

I moved away, commonsense prevailing inside me, the consequences of a collision with his rushing body too bruising to contemplate. I shook my head, in admiration or maybe exasperation.

Now his swing was so wide that his body was horizontal at the end of each arc, and although the stretched tendons in his neck audibly twanged even over the roar of the storm, I knew he still wasn't dead, that in fact he had no intention of permitting himself to die until he was quite ready. The futility of the stunt appalled me, the faith he had placed in a possibly fake legend, in muttered beery words in a dim room.

'Uncle Dylan, this is your fault!' I hissed, as I turned to look back at a dark façade, the hotel without a single lit window, the panes of glass like fossilised eyelids, a cold hive of insane rumours.

Matthew Loveday was now close to achieving the highest ambition of any amateur swinger, the complete loop. It was clear that this had been a part of the scheme all along, his and the wind's.

I fell to my knees in the grass, privileged to be a witness.

Then it happened. Lightning photographed the event, a perfect circle, a wheel with a single half-alive spoke; and gathering momentum, he looped the loop again, and then a third time, until like a motor cranked into life he began spinning at a dizzying rate, the dreadfully fascinating afterimage of his suicide becoming a disc with a solid rim.

The base of the tree began to shift in its setting, rocking slightly every time he passed, working itself loose, almost as if brass screws had jumped free from an engine block, and moist black earth around the roots bubbled and trickled like water down the side of the mound. I started laughing and pointing and reeling, briefly mad, for I guessed exactly what was going to happen. The legend was about to destroy itself.

Matthew Loveday was now whirling at such a ferocious velocity that I supposed he had reinforced his neck somehow, perhaps by swallowing a hollow metal tube. Decapitation would have been assured otherwise. The roots of the tree were almost fully exposed now and the soil of the mound was crumbling fast around them as the trunk jerked violently from side to side, a rotten tooth wobbling in diseased gums.

Another flash of lightning blinded me. In the darkness that followed a heartbeat later, I heard a dreadful sucking sound.

My vision cleared. The tree was gone. I looked up and saw it rising, a wooden rocket pulled by an inverted man towards the zenith, applauded magisterially by the loudest peal of thunder yet.

The Swinger

Then it vanished between muddy clouds. The rain whipped at my face, as if to punish it for an act of unknown insolence, and I exhaled all the air in my lungs, deflating my body and my mind.

Something fell back, a clod of earth or black stone and bounced across the lawns like a bomb, but it didn't explode. It tumbled into bushes but I watched it only from the corner of one eye. My attention was focussed on the closed clouds, those drawn curtains of brown and grey clotted vapour, a veil thick enough to smother as well as conceal.

And then, as I had expected and hoped and dreaded, they parted again to return the tree to its sessile roost, to drop it vertically like a sepia film in reverse into the gaping socket where it had stood. It bored through the mound, a gigantic flechette, and completely vanished into the soft earth. I lurched forward on legs stiffened by the electric current in the air, scaled the crumbling slope with considerable difficulty.

The tree had buried itself. Albino mists drifted limply out of the hole it had made, the pit that led down into the centre of the mound, from which a length of rope also straggled, thick rope with a rough itchy noose at the exposed end. I saw this when I reeled it in.

Then I sat down on the cold steam and laughed.

The tightened noose was empty.

I walked back to the hotel with a lowered head. I felt at that moment that I would never be able to lift it again, that it was safer to proceed through life with my chin on my chest, to prevent any noose being placed around *my* neck, whether by my own hand or through the malice of others. When I passed through the broken doorway, I forgot this fear. The dying storm was moving away, taking madness with it.

There was a shuffling at the top of the stairs and a figure moved in the overlapping cones of wan light from a candlestick with two branches and two stubs of sputtering tallow jammed into it. 'The storm has brought the power lines down,' said a sleepy voice. 'We have been plunged into the past but nobody asked for our permission.'

'A cliché,' I answered him, but without a sneer.

Uncle Dylan was dressed in comical style, with a spotted red nightcap so long it hung down to his waist and striped yellow pyjamas that clashed with it so horribly I was convinced a nasty joke was being played, that the events of the night had been manufactured.

'Is it worth going outside? I'll have to get my slippers.'

'Do they have curly toes?' I sighed.

He nodded and I began tramping up the stairs towards him, partly to ensure he would retreat, for there wasn't enough room for two to pass. I stood before him on the landing and rested one arm on his shoulder and then I told him what had happened, that Loveday was dead, that his body might have come down on a neighbouring property, possibly without his head, which would land somewhere else.

'Can you be certain about any of this?' he retorted.

There was a note of weary aggression in his voice that baffled me, as if he considered me too stubborn to learn an obvious lesson. We regarded each other with shocked hostility for half a minute, then he softened and in the dropped light as one of the candle flames died he said, 'Let's fetch beer for ourselves. We deserve it, don't we?'

'First we should look into his room,' I replied.

Uncle Dylan shrugged. Matthew Loveday had occupied a space in one of the many haphazard extensions that had been added to the edifice over the years. It was triangular in shape with a warped ceiling and suitable for any dreamer who equated impractical with quaint. The door was shut but unlocked and we crowded inside and frowned, disapproving inspectors of geometry and clutter, the leavings of a life.

'He used a typewriter, do you believe it? The stubborn fool.'

'A romantic,' corrected Uncle Dylan.

'There's a sheet of paper in the machine. Step closer.'

Uncle Dylan pulled it out, forgetting to operate the release mechanism and tearing the page slightly. It was a letter addressed to him. Licking his lips, he gave it to me and held the sickly flame at an angle, dripping wax onto the bare floorboards with an audible and regular click, like a rain of insects. 'I don't like reading,' he grumbled.

I recited it softly in the still air of the doomed man's room, in that old and infinitely lonely isosceles of futile dreams. I spoke as if I really was Matthew Loveday and my voice changed, adopted his accent and pauses, his timorous yet determined tone. Uncle Dylan shut his eyes, swaying and nodding but keeping the candle flame steady.

'I always knew,' I began, 'that one day I would sit down and write a suicide note but this isn't it, so don't squeeze sad expressions from your face too hard or you might damage a muscle. There's no need for either of us to feel awkward. Your company was enjoyable enough but I won't miss it too much because I don't belong in this *time*. The modern world disgusts me, so I've decided to take a gamble on the truth of the legend you told me and hang myself into another age.

'It's a desperate measure, but if it doesn't work I won't notice, and if it does I'll be free, at least as free as anyone has ever been, for it might be the case that freedom itself is an illusion. No matter. I intend to stay alive if I can, but not in this century. I choose to go back to the era that my new novel is set in, the Dark Ages right here at this precise site, just before the founding of the monastery, if that structure ever existed. I want to live for real the daydreams that I have turned into prose.

'My novel was carefully researched, but how can it be accurate when so little is known about that period of history? In fact it's safer to say that this part of Wales in the seventh century was *outside* history altogether. I know there are absurdities in my book, incorrect patterns and behaviours, catastrophes of detail, solecisms, other errors. I'll correct them if I can. If I do establish myself among the local people without being pitch-forked to death I will rewrite my novel, but more faithfully.

'When it is done, I'll waterproof it most carefully, wrap it in layers of skins and seal it in a box, closing all air holes with resin. Then I'll bury it at the top of the sacred mound and plant a tree there, a cedar, the very tree that has haunted you for so long. Look for the box, open it, and offer what you find to my publisher as a superior second edition. Of course all this is a long shot, but what's so fine about short shots? I might even end up as a ghost in your hotel, the one that haunted myself. . . .'

I finished and allowed the letter to slide out of my hand and glide into the shadows. Uncle Dylan cleared his throat. 'He asked about ghosts but never said anything about being haunted himself. Maybe he thought the correct etiquette was to suffer in silence?'

'Not all hauntings are unpleasant,' I answered.

'But by his own ghost? Ugh!'

'If he *had* been haunted by himself, that would have given him plenty of encouragement that he did succeed in travelling into the past. It makes a dreadful kind of sense,' I conceded.

'What shall we do now? The box?'

'It must have been entangled in the roots of the tree. I saw something fall out of the sky. It's worth a quick search.'

60

The Swinger

We should have waited until morning, of course, but I was too eager to prove or disprove the outrageous conclusion to the entire adventure. Rain and wind had dropped to a minimum, but Uncle Dylan's candle still went out. It didn't matter. On hands and knees I fumbled in the bushes, pulled out the worn box, mud-spattered, decaying.

Curiously warm to the touch it was, as well, and I took it inside before opening it with a chisel. Under layers of mouldy skins a pallid manuscript gleamed at us. I picked it up and it didn't crumble. The ink was faded but legible and the language was modern English.

'You do realise the whole thing could be a hoax?' I said.

'That would be even more farfetched.'

'Yes, I guess so. I think I'll start reading it now, but I haven't read the first version yet. Does it matter, I wonder?'

Uncle Dylan shrugged. He was good at shrugging. A notable shrugger in any situation that required one. He went to pour beer and brought me a full glass of thick black foam and I sipped. He drank his own glass faster and soon went for a refill, and then another.

He eventually guzzled enough and left me alone. I kept turning pages and moving my moist lips as I read; it seemed more respectful. The tale was enthralling and presumably extremely accurate, a superb evocation of life as it had been back then. The irony was that the publisher eventually rejected it as a replacement for the original.

'An inferior and implausible rewrite,' was his judgment. He reprinted the first edition and I returned from my fruitless trip to London with sighs stuck in my throat like unripe cherries. When I reached the hotel I learned that Uncle Dylan had acquired a new guest.

'Jerome Nightjar,' with an unconvincing flourish.

'Will you be staying long?' I asked.

'I hope so. Months,' he replied.

'He's very similar to Matthew,' Uncle Dylan whispered to me, 'and I have given him the triangular room.'

He wore casual but smart clothes with a pale blue shirt missing the top buttons. There was a scorch mark around his throat as if friction had done him a recent disservice. I wondered about the inhabitants who had greeted Matthew Loveday all those centuries ago, who had beheld a similar mark on his neck but who tolerated his presence anyway, even allowing him to plant a tree on the summit of a sacred mound.

'Oh yes! We have a ghost,' Uncle Dylan was saying in his usual bluff manner; and I snapped back to the present.

Jerome Nightjar grinned immensely.

A large bird flew past the window. I waved at it.

AN INCOMPLETE APOCALYPSE
Mark Valentine

'I think you make out your case quite well,' conceded Burns, leaning back in his crimson leather armchair 'but there's something missing that would really clinch it.'

Hugo Winwick gazed across at him with pale, silvery eyes, and made a noise indicative of polite curiosity.

They were discussing his paper on later medieval English apocalypses, submitted to the journal *The Hourglass*. It was a respectable place to be published, and Winwick was quite keen to appear there. In looking at illustrated manuscript volumes of the Revelation of St John the Divine, he had, some months ago, experienced his own minor revelation. He had begun to speculate that there had been a turning point in the production of these vivid apocalypses, when they were no longer made mainly for *pious* use, but simply as aesthetic objects, as ornamental books. They had moved from the preserve of the abbot, the prior and the bishop to that of the courtier, even the dilettante. Noble and gentle folk, he contended, had them made simply because they liked looking at fiery monsters. It could be seen, if you liked, as a first surging of the longing for the Gothic in the human spirit: an important new artistic thesis.

Winwick was fairly certain that in his specialist field this was quite a new line to suggest, and he wanted to get his work known soon, in some authoritative venue. Up until then, the assumption had been made that any illuminated and calligraphic text on a biblical theme (and there were hardly any others) had been painstakingly produced by monks in their scriptoria for the edification of zealous patrons, keen to study scripture in handsome volumes. Yet he had found, by a fresh scrutiny of several fragmentary examples, that in later years, just before the dawn of printing, many had been made by skilled, *secular* scribes: artisans, creating their work for worldly and wealthy clients who simply wanted something luxurious and magnificent to feast their eyes upon—and, no doubt, to flaunt at their neighbours and visitors.

'Yes,' the editor of *The Hourglass* continued, 'what you need to find is an apocalypse completely out of any churchly context. I'm quite persuaded by your line of thought, but in each example you've found, a conventional religious motive *might* still be possible. If you could find and describe one that was bound up only with purely literary or scholarly pages—oh, legends, fabulous histories, almanacs, that kind of thing—your argument would be so much more powerful.'

'Yes, I quite see that,' his would-be contributor agreed. 'And I'm convinced some must exist. But I haven't come across one yet. We'll have to do without. Unless you have any ideas?'

Burns seemed to hesitate, and began to scrape his pipe out with a silver device designed for this purpose. This was evidently a sign that he wanted to think. The scraping marked out the silence like a clock's ticking. At last he paused, and looked at Winwick in a sideways sort of way.

'We-ll. There certainly is a likely contender. The Draycott. Do you know it?'

'The Draycott Apocalypse?' The name murmured at the back of Winwick's mind, though he could not say quite why.

'Yes. Incomplete, of course. But they so often are.'

'Pages sold off to collectors by indigent owner?' asked Winwick, to show that he knew the way of these things.

'No doubt.'

But the author felt an unusual quiver of frankness pass through him.

'I don't know much about it, I'm afraid,' he confessed.

Winwick was hesitant in admitting to this deficiency in his learning to the notoriously severe editor. But to his relief Burns shook his head.

'I'm not at all surprised. It's never been written up. But from what I understand, it's bound up with all sorts of other stuff, not in the least pious. That might be the lead you need.'

He agreed, keenly.

'We've had a few chaps in the past offer to do a feature on it, as it happens. I even gave them introductions to the owner. It's supposed to be quite fine, what's left anyway. But for one reason or another, they never did send me a paper. Flighty blighters, I expect, who liked the idea of getting their name in, but couldn't be bothered to put in the fieldwork.'

He cocked a sardonic eyebrow, and blew lustily into the pipe bowl, as if scattering such idle defaulters to the winds, with the dead ashes.

Winwick took the hint.

Before pursuing the obscure apocalypse further, Hugo elicited from the editor the names of the two young scholars who had each raised with him the idea of writing an article about it. And then he checked various digests and catalogues to ensure that they had not, in fact, already written up the book in some *other* journal, spurning Burns: he would look foolish if he had been forestalled. But there was no sign whatever of any work of this kind: and, indeed, no sign whatever of the supposed authors, so that Winwick began to wonder if the editor of *The Hourglass* might have got their names wrong. However, when he asked amongst some of his academic acquaintances, he found that a few had indeed heard, rather vaguely, of the two young antiquarians, though none recently. Some wondered if they had been lured by American universities.

'Yes, they've probably gone off to the New World,' said one, old McGibbon. 'Warmer climes and brighter sparks and all that.'

Winwick had, anyway, satisfied himself that he would certainly be amongst the first to write up the Draycott Apocalypse, and he composed and addressed a formal letter asking for permission to view the book. It was still, it seemed, in the ownership of the country family who had given their name to the work. He hoped he had offered the appropriate mingling of authority and deference in his application: the college arms upon the notepaper, and some mild flattery about the family's dedicated guardianship of so important a relic. And it seemed that he had: an invitation promptly followed. The Draycotts, of Draycott Hall, in the village, or rather hamlet of Draycott (for there appeared to be no church), in some dim region of Northamptonshire, seemed to have dwindled to a single scion, named by Burns as Miss Lily Draycott. He had given her first name with a slight sneering hiss, as if he did not quite approve, perhaps because it had, in his day, been bestowed upon actresses and courtesans.

The place was, at least, only a fairly short journey from Winwick's college, but it was a dispiriting one, through wan fenland, and across low, dun, ridges faint against a dwindling winter sky. There was no-one to meet him at the station, but the directions supplied, in a hand of rather quavery dark ink, showed that he had a walk of about forty minutes ahead of him. There was a chill breeze to face, which bit at the delicate spirals of his ears, and whetted its teeth too on his rather austere nose.

He strode on as resolutely as he could, and all around saw only frosted fields and hedgerows, coated with a clinging white fire.

The hall, when at length it glimmered into view in a sort of dreary haze across descending moorland, was of a pale, friable, weathered stone, and as he approached Winwick found himself thinking that it looked almost as if its very walls had been made of timeworn parchment: there was the same dry, dusty appearance. It stood far back from the nearest road, behind a screen of larch trees, whose thin limbs rattled in the bitter air.

Most of the windows, on the three rather squatting storeys that could be made out, still wore shutters, scarred by the winds and with paint peeling in grey flakes, as if they were the scales of some creature sloughing off old skin as it slept. The doorway was not a grand gesture, as so often in country houses, but a simple, low, almost square dark slot in the walls. Winwick looked about, but there appeared to be no bell, only a brass knocker rimed with a green crust, in a twisted shape that might have been intended once for an elephant's trunk. Perhaps, Winwick reflected, one of the Draycotts had been a servant of the empire and had installed this curio as a remembrance. He seized the brazen coil, which, despite the bleak wind, had a tingle of warmth to it, as if it had caught the rays of an unseen sun, and rapped it against the door.

The woman who answered his hollow knock after a short echoing silence wore a long dark gown relieved only by a scarlet, silken sash around her waist, from which depended a peal of silver and bronze keys. It was difficult to tell her age from her appearance: there were no obvious signs of wear in the amber-tinted skin of her long face, and her eyes still seemed to have a lively glimmer. But a great tower of silvery-black hair suggested the passage of a certain number of years, at least. She gestured to him to follow her along a stone passageway, and ushered him into a bare parlour where a table was carefully set out for a meal. He had not been certain at first whether he had been met by a housekeeper, or the chatelaine herself, and had proceeded with circumspection: but his doubts were resolved when she proffered her hand, elaborately festooned with gems, and he gave this the briefest of touches. She gestured him to a chair, and poured a dank wine into the glass before him. Then she signalled with a fluttering motion, almost like a blessing, over the silver chafing-dishes, and they helped themselves. When the genteel scraping and clattering had subsided, his host addressed him once more.

'We are extra parochial, you understand.'

He could certainly imagine that the obscurity of the place would make its inhabitants more than usually interested only in their own local affairs, but it seemed an odd beginning.

Her black, glistening eyes, rather like skinned grapes, detected his confusion.

'I mean that we do not here belong to any parish—we are quite free from all civic or ecclesiastical interference. Usually that is only the case where the land formerly belonged to an abbey or to the throne. But here, neither ever applied. So it is not clear to historians why we have been left alone.'

There was almost a melancholy fall to her last words, and her eyes glinted in the glow from the corroded candlesticks. Her long fingers, ornamented with the many bizarre rings, which were twisted like serpents around the waxen sticks of flesh, wafted once more in the dim light.

'In those days, Mr Wanwick, it was said men feared the Church, the King and the Devil, in that order. Since we have never had any very obvious affinity with the first two, it has sometimes been supposed that we must have thrown in our lot with the, ah, *junior* partner—d'you see?'

She laughed to herself, in a series of throaty surges that were not unlike a purring.

Her visitor smiled weakly.

'Actually, it's Winwick,' he murmured. But his hostess appeared not to hear him.

'Be that as it may, if we can hardly say that we have ever *flourished* as a family, yet we have at least enjoyed a long decay.'

Winwick felt these phrases had been deployed before.

'Charming place . . . warm welcome,' he muttered. His feeble remarks went unregarded.

'You know the meddler, Mr Wanwick?' he heard her ask.

Her guest cast about anxiously in his mind for any of his acquaintances who might be regarded as unusually meddlesome. Perhaps Burns was meant, who had put him in touch?

'Well, I . . .'

'The *medlar* fruit. It may only be taken when it is in decay. And then, I say, a very noble taste: autumn leaves and sweet dates. We nurture it here. In the old orchard.'

There was a slight emphasis on the word *old*, as if to imply that there had been many other fruit groves since this original.

Winwick expressed polite interest, but this was lost in the next remark.

'As with that rare fruit, so with some old families, perhaps. Finest in decay.'

It was difficult to know how to respond with politeness to this, without admitting either that he discerned the decay or that he disputed the fineness, so Hugo Winwick allowed a silence to elapse, before attempting the brief speech of thanks he had mentally composed and refined on his train journey and on the brisk walk from the station.

'. . . particularly as I understand you have already given your most generous hospitality to scholars before me. . . .'

Dark World

Miss Draycott had been regarding him with the sort of amused and inquisitive look one might bestow upon a pet that has learnt a new and slightly unexpected trick, until he petered out with this final remark.

She sighed, disturbing the candles, whose amber flames flickered as if shrinking back in dismay.

'Perhaps you would like to go to the *Revelation* now, Mr Wanwick?'

Miss Draycott rose, with a rustle of her dress, which had the dark polish of old mahogany. The pleats seemed to shimmer in the candlelight like black flames.

The manuscript was kept in a casket in an upper room, which had a single arched window. It was barely furnished with a riddled wooden table and a chair whose legs ended in worn claws. And it was cold: the bleak wind that had assailed him on his walk to the hall was not kept out here, but seemed to whisper and moan in the crevices of the walls. He rubbed his fingers together, and carefully raised the great dark binding of the book before him.

As Burns had surmised, the book was indeed bound up with other, wholly secular material. So far as Winwick could make out, on a first rapid examination, there was, firstly, some sort of treatise on orchardry, full of the shapes of trees that he certainly did not recognise, some bearing fruit that appeared to possess the ability to grimace and stare; then a herball, among whose illustrations he noticed a mandrake, a moly, and a monkshood, together with stranger blooms still, with limbs like twisted homunculi; and then a set of pages indited with archaic symbols, angular and, as it were, stalking over the page. There was perhaps a hint of Hebrew in their calligraphy, or some even older language, which he did not now have the time more thoroughly to examine. And then, at last, as he turned the pages ever more eagerly, there came the apocalypse itself, and Winwick dwelled upon each leaf with wonder. This was one of the most strongly imagined he had ever seen.

The figures had been drawn in fine black ink first, and the colour added by means of a tinted wash. This was, he knew, a special craft secret of English illuminators, more subtle than the smears of raw pigment used elsewhere. It was particularly suitable, Winwick noticed, to depict the proper colour of an English sea: the grey-green was admirably achieved, and much more realistic than the bright blaring blue of convention, which might just about do for the Mediterranean. It was a delicate, careful art, which seemed apt for the limners at work in a rainwashed and misty island. He turned the pages with a quick delight, the zeal of the scholar leaping up inside him, and the desire to be the first chronicler of this exquisite masterpiece crackling within him.

The realism had also been applied, he thought, to the rather splendid seven-headed, crowned and horned serpent or dragon. It looked like something that just might have been drawn out from the dreary depths of some English fen to confront and carry off all the kingdom's sinners. Despite its beady eyes and lashing red tongues, its slime-coloured scales and spurred wings, there was just the faintest air of melancholy to it. He looked at the human figure painted as if writhing before the monster. Perhaps, he thought, rather too irreverently, the beast was disappointed because its prey did not have a face that it could threaten.

For here was one part where the Draycott Apocalypse, which otherwise seemed remarkably intact, was indeed incomplete. There were no features on the believer confronted by the dragon with seven heads: everything else was limned in, their body, limbs, clothes, shoes, and they were even depicted under a withered black fig tree, but they had no face. For some reason the artist had simply stopped short.

Winwick looked at the pale oval carefully, bringing his gaze close to it, in case he could detect any signs of erasure. There were very slight, minute ripples in the paper, which for a moment gave the impression of quivering. He narrowed his eyes and stared even more intently. Was there the merest hint of a skein of flesh coloured in there, or was that the fading of the manuscript? But, yes, the pink tint began to seem more substantial, and he even felt he could discern the smudges of eyes, ears and nose. He drew back, to look away and give his eyes a rest, blinking. And then he regarded the picture once more. The seven-headed monster in its hues of English mud and rain and marsh still glimmered upon the page, and its victim's clothes had their autumn hues of scarlet and gold and brown. But the white void, the solemn blank mask, on top of the figure's shoulders, indeed seemed much more defined now. It was certainly possible to make out the lineaments of some of the features. The eyes were a wan grey, the ears rather like delicate shells, and the nose, narrow and sensitive. As if in a paper mirror, Hugo Winwick found himself staring at his own face.

Something that might have been the wind roared among the walls of the room.

FIRST NIGHT
Anna Taborska

They chased the fleeing girl relentlessly, their horses snorting and sweating in the sultry air. Sooner or later they would catch her— she knew that, and headed for the lake at the edge of the village. For a while she lost her pursuers among the dense trees. A fresh wave of tears stained her youthful face as she burst out onto the bank. There she paused a moment, trying to catch her breath amidst the beauty of the desolate place with its vast expanse of dark water and row of weeping willows, their leaves rustling uneasily as she moved past them towards the water's edge. She could hear the shouts and the thunder of hooves coming closer. Dizzy with fear and exhaustion, she leaned for a moment against a willow tree. Then, casting a glance over her shoulder, she threw herself forward. In that final second, her thoughts turned to her beloved. Her heart was broken even before the dark waters closed over her head.

The willow trailed its leaves in the water like verdant tears. Its branches stirred restlessly as the horse and cart struggled past, headed for the village guest house.

'Splendid!' remarked Henry, looking in the direction of the lake. Dan followed his gaze, expecting to spy some new marvel amidst the stunning rural landscape, but instead saw two local girls, one with long brown hair plaited down her back and the other wearing a traditional flowery headscarf. Henry waved at them, and they waved back, giggling. He turned to his companion. 'I think we're in there, old man,' he informed Dan with a grin.

'Right,' Dan was unconvinced. Then again, the ladies seemed to go for Henry's ex public school charms, and, the two of them being exotic foreigners, even Dan was getting a bit of female attention.

'Aren't you glad we didn't take a cab after all!' It was a statement rather than a question, but Dan felt that a response was expected nonetheless.

'Right,' he agreed uncertainly and tightened his grip on the side of the cart, his eyes glued to the peasant's back and the horse's rump beyond. Dan came from a stalwart middle class family in Birmingham, and horses were not something he'd ever planned on getting this close to. But Henry was evidently loving the whole Eastern European thing. Dan couldn't help but wonder how strange it was that Henry of all people—Henry who, despite his foreign surname, was to all intents and purposes more English than the Queen—should go haring around Poland, looking for traces of his ancestors. Still and all, perhaps it was less un-PC than exploring the colonialist past on his mother's side. In any case, Dan enjoyed Henry's company and was happy to tag along.

Eventually the road led away from the lake and uphill a little. The horse snorted and strained onwards, foamy sweat dripping from its sides. Dan sighed with relief as the cart rolled to a halt outside the quaint old building that served as the local guesthouse.

'Good evening,' the receptionist smiled at Henry in a manner that Dan was beginning to find a little annoying.

Several hours and a considerable number of vodkas later, Dan turned up the Polish sitcom on his TV in a vain attempt to drown out the sounds of Henry entertaining the receptionist in the room next door. Henry and Dan had dined together, then sat at the hotel bar, where the receptionist doubled as barmaid. The two Brits seemed to be the only visitors at the small guest-house, and Henry had taken advantage of the lack of other customers to persuade the Polish girl to join them in a few drinks. Eventually Dan had made his excuses and gone up to his room, leaving Henry and the girl to their own devices. It hadn't been long, however, before he'd heard them entering Henry's room.

Dan flicked through the channels, trying to find something he could actually watch, but even the American blockbusters had a lector reading the Polish translation over the English dialogue in a way that rendered both languages less than audible. He turned off the TV. Dan became aware of the wind sighing outside his window. He opened it wide and leaned out. From his vantage point on the top floor he could see the lake along which they had travelled on their way to the hotel. From what Dan had worked out, it formed part of an extensive complex of lakes and waterways, stretching for miles, many of them hidden among the dense forest that still covered this part of the country. The lake was surrounded by trees—willows by the looks of them—which glowed a pale silver in the moonlight and rustled in the wind that animated their branches. Dan shivered and closed the window. When he finally fell asleep, his dreams were disturbing, alien.

The girl's beauty was spoken of even beyond the village bounda-ries. She could have had any of the local youths, but she chose the blacksmith's son. Her mother's bakery stood opposite the smithy, and she had frequently watched the young man helping his father shoe horses. While the blacksmith nailed on the iron shoes, his son tended the beasts, rubbing their tired legs and speaking to them gently. The couple fell in love, and their parents saw no reason to stand in the way of their happiness. Their wedding was not grand, but the whole village turned out, and the sun shone brightly for the bride and groom. But their joy was not to last long.

As was the custom, the lord of the manor had been invited to the wedding feast. As was his *custom, the lord had failed to turn up. Then, just as the sun was beginning to dip behind the trees, and the newlyweds were starting to wonder when they would be able to slip away from the festivities, the assembled villagers heard excited shouts and the sound of horses' hooves approaching rapidly.*

'Good evening!' It was the lord of the manor and a rowdy party of his companions. He jumped off his horse and his fellows followed suit. The villagers rose from the tables around which they were seated, bowing and curtsying to the newcomers. 'We shan't be staying,' informed the lord, 'we've just come for the bride.' A stunned silence fell on the wedding party, broken only by the drunken guffaws of the lord's companions. The girl's already pale face turned as white as her bridal gown, and she looked to her husband for protection. The blacksmith's son stood rooted to the spot, and the lord addressed the girl. 'Don't look so frightened, my dear; I daresay we shan't do anything you haven't done before!'

'Please, my lord,' a woman's voice rose from the crowd. 'She's a good girl . . . a virgin.' The lord was caught off guard for a moment, then spotted the girl's mother, and laughed.

'A virgin?'

'Yes, my lord.' The nobleman exchanged amused glances with his companions, then turned his attention back to the girl's mother.

First Night

'All the better, woman. I'll teach her everything she needs to know to please her husband . . . tomorrow night.' The lord glanced at his cronies again, and they obliged with peels of raucous laughter.

'Please, my love,' the girl took her husband's hand and whispered urgently to him as the young lord toyed with her mother. 'Let's slip out the back. They're drunk. We'll take a horse and ride away. By tomorrow he'll have lost interest.' Her husband looked at her sadly, but made no response. 'Please, let's go. You are my only one. I'd rather die than lie with another.'

'It is his right,' the blacksmith's son finally replied. Those quietly spoken words shattered the girl's world. Tears welling up in her eyes, she pulled her hand from her husband's and fled from her wedding table. It took a moment for the lord to notice that his prize was gone.

'Well, what are you waiting for?' he shouted to his companions, angry and amused in equal measure. 'Bring her back!'

The following morning, armed with a map and directions from the somewhat embarrassed receptionist, Henry and Dan set off in search of Henry's ancestral home. Henry seemed uncannily refreshed, considering how much vodka and how little sleep he'd had, and it was Dan who felt tired and uneasy. He still had vague memories of a bizarre dream he'd had—of the weeping willows that grew along the lake coming alive and forming a circle around him, trapping him and closing in on him. It was all he could do to keep up with his energetic friend.

The guesthouse that Henry had chosen—not that there was much choosing to do, it being the only one in the area—was not far from the manor house that had once belonged to Henry's ancestors. So the two young men set off on foot, following the road along the large lake. Dan avoided looking at the willows, gazing instead at the open fields on the opposite side of the road.

Eventually the lake curved away to the right. Henry and Dan kept to the road, and carried on straight ahead until they came across a large dilapidated stone gatepost to their left. A couple of metres away, obscured by brambles, stood a second gatepost.

'This is it,' Henry grinned at Dan and turned off the road. As they passed between the two posts, they paused in wonder. Ahead of them stretched an avenue of ancient linden trees, seeming to go on forever. The friends exchanged awed glances, then headed up the avenue. Eventually they could make out a large grassy area with a circular grey stone structure in the distance, and beyond that the red bricks of a building. As Henry and Dan approached the end of the avenue, their excitement grew. Finally they were out of the shade of the trees and in the open: in what had once been a large courtyard. Even now, overgrown with grass on which a cow was grazing, the courtyard was impressive. The circular stone structure in the centre of it was an old fountain—cracked and drained of water, the dry leaves inside it crackling in a breeze that stirred as the young men walked past. Something about the broken, empty structure unnerved Dan. Beyond the fountain and the courtyard stood the manor house. The render had long since fallen off, revealing the red brick that Henry and Dan had seen from the avenue. But the manor was still a thing of beauty. The main building was a vast rectangular block. On either side of it a curved colonnade led to a smaller, cube-like building. Together, the central block with its two wings formed a perfect horseshoe.

From what Henry had managed to find out while researching for their trip, the stately home was the work of an Italian architect—an unsung genius—who had been brought to Poland by a wealthy Polish count for the sole purpose of building him a palace fit for a king. The Italian had subsequently returned to Italy, where he was killed in a bar brawl in a village inn. The manor had since withstood attacks by Cossacks, Tartars and a variety of other hostile foreigners, before finally falling victim— in 1945—to the Polish Communist Security Agency, whose officers set fire to the main building on account of a unit of anti-Communist Polish Home Army partisans hiding within its walls. The partially burnt-out shell of the manor remained and, in a humorously symbolic act of class-war—the intentionality of which would never be known for sure—local representatives of the Polish People's Workers' Party used it to house pigs. By the 1980s the porkers too were gone, and the manor remained in the derelict state in which the two young Brits now found it. The roof had caved in—in places, and here and there a shattered roof-tile lay upon the ground.

'So this belonged to your great grandfather?' asked Dan, impressed.

'And to his great grandfather before him,' grinned Henry. 'You never know, with the Commies gone, maybe my dad can claim it back or something!' Henry moved towards the main entrance. 'Come on!'

The front door was gone without a trace, and the two friends entered slowly, careful not to fall down a hole—of which there were many. There were piles of rubble lying around, the obligatory quasi-Satanist graffiti on the walls, and two vast, symmetrically positioned spiral staircases, but no banisters. After an inspection of the ground-floor rooms, which revealed the odd partially standing chimney-breast and more graffiti, the two friends headed cautiously up the stairs. The first floor was equally devastated, with bird droppings beneath the gaping holes that had once been the windows. Dan was already slowly mounting the stairs to the second floor, when Henry spotted a doorway to a room that he hadn't noticed before.

'Go on up,' he told Dan. 'I'll be along in a minute. Just be careful.'

'Okay. You too.'

The second floor laid bare the full extent of the damage to the roof. It was dark here, despite the daylight outside, and, the ceiling long being gone, shafts of light fell through the many holes and cracks in the roof. Motes of dust danced and glistened in the shafts, mesmerising Dan for a moment. Then, feeling uneasy alone in the vast dark space, he moved cautiously to one of the windows and peered out. He caught sight of movement and panicked on seeing figures in the park at the back of the building. He moved back a step—out of the light—but, on looking out again, realised that they were willow trees, hunched over like people. Unnerved, Dan called out to Henry, then went back down to the first floor to look for him.

'Henry?' No answer. Not finding him on the first floor, Dan carefully descended the less damaged spiral staircase. 'Henry!' Dan figured that his friend must have gone back out—perhaps to explore the two wings of the palace—although Dan couldn't understand why he hadn't said anything.

But the buildings on either side of the main house were locked, and Henry was nowhere to be seen. There was only one place left to check, and that was the park behind the palace.

'Henry!' But there was no sign of Henry in the park either. As Dan turned back towards the manor, he thought he saw movement in one of the windows. 'Oh, for God's sake . . . Henry!' Maybe his friend hadn't left the building after all, but then why hadn't he answered Dan's calls?

Dan walked quickly back to the house. There was no sign of anyone in the window now, but Dan was determined to go in for another look. As he reached the back of the house and started to head towards the colonnade, planning to cut through under its arches and go back into the house, he felt a sudden rush of air, then a sharp pain on the side of his head, and he was out cold.

Her heart was broken even before the dark waters closed over her head. She didn't struggle as her heavy garments took on water and pulled her down to the muddy bottom of the deep lake. She sank slowly—like a thousand broken-hearted maidens before her —and the willows wept beside her watery bed.

A brief moment of panic, as the girl's last breath escaped her; then a blissful stillness enveloped her, and a profound sense of serenity and peace.

Dan awoke to something wet and malodorous brushing against his face. The cow that had been grazing round the front of the manor house had wandered over and—whether for lack of salt in its diet or for some unfathomable bovine reason of its own— was now licking the prostrate young man. Dan jumped up and the startled cow beat a hasty retreat, mooing in alarm. Dan nearly blacked out again, and sat back down, breathing deeply. There was a dull throbbing pain in his temples and a much sharper pain at the side of his head when he touched it. He also had an impressive lump where the tile had struck. Unbeknown to Dan, his luck was in. Had the roof-tile hit him full-on, rather than just skimming the side of his head, he would not be getting up again.

Dan shivered, and realised that the air had grown much colder; indeed—the sun was already going down. Alarmed at how much time must have passed, Dan called out to his friend. He suddenly felt afraid for Henry, but tried to console himself with the thought that Henry must have become carried away exploring somewhere in the house or vast grounds, and that he simply couldn't hear him calling. Dan got up—slowly this time —and made his way cautiously under the arches of the colonnade and back to the house, staying away from the eaves as much as he could.

Although the sun had not quite set, the shadows inside the manor were profound. Dan had planned to go all around the house again in search of his friend, but remembered the treacherous staircase and damaged floor, and thought better of it. Instead he peered into the darkness from the threshold, and called Henry's name loudly. No response. Only the slight movement of shifting rubble somewhere in the depths of the building—too soft to be made by a man. Rats perhaps? Or just the house readjusting to the drop in temperature? But there was that feeling of dread in the pit of Dan's stomach again—fear of being left alone in this strange, abandoned place, but an even stronger fear for his friend.

'Henry!' Nothing. Dan touched his aching head gently, winced, then set off through the courtyard, hoping to do a large loop in front of the house before returning to the back and carrying out a thorough search of the gardens while there was still sufficient daylight. But as he walked past the fountain, something didn't seem right—something on the periphery of his vision. Dan stopped abruptly, and glanced to the right. That's when he saw the dark shape.

'Christ!' Dan's heart leapt in his chest, and for a moment he thought he might pass out again. He calmed himself as best he could, but the longer he stared at the thing in the fountain, the more details he noticed: the blue jeans, the navy sweatshirt, the dark blonde hair . . . yes, it was hair. There was no doubt now in Dan's mind. Lying in the cracked old fountain was a body, and the closer he got to it, the more certain he was that it was that of his friend.

A rough, scratching sensation roused the girl from her murky grave. She felt a sharp tug, then another and another. Then coarse limbs were holding her, and gnarled digits curled around her body. She was being lifted, pulled and dragged—upwards and out and away from the death-bringing, peace-bringing water.

As she felt solid ground beneath her feet once more, the girl's feet began to crack. On all sides the willow trees that cradled her started to grow over and into and through her body. Roots moved through her legs and feet, shackling her to the earth. Her fingers grew long and brittle; her skin hardened, thickened and erupted in shoots and stems, which shivered in the evening air. The girl tried to move, but her legs were rooted to the spot and her torso trapped in a wooden corset that held her fast. Her eyes became hollow, her throat twisted and dry. She screamed, and her cry froze forever onto the rugged bark of her lips.

All memories fled the girl, bar those of sadness and longing, betrayal and anger, and a need for revenge stronger than hunger or thirst—stronger than the centuries that would come and go.

The minutes and days that followed could only be described as a never-ending nightmare. . . . Touching his friend's ice-cold neck to check for a pulse; the glazed, milky eye that stared up at him from under Henry's matted hair; stumbling back to the guest-house through the dark. Then the uncomprehending, shocked face of the receptionist; the police; the ambulance; the battery of questions and suspicious looks. But the worst thing was seeing Henry's parents: his mother trembling like a leaf in a gale, his father ashen-faced and trying to be strong for his wife.

'What happened, Dan?'

Dark World

'I don't know. I . . . don't . . . know.'

Dan went over the events of that day a hundred times: with Henry's parents, with the police, when he lay awake at night. But nobody would ever know why it was that Henry's lungs were filled with water or how it was that a young man could drown in the long-empty shell of a cracked old fountain.

By the time the men reached the lake, there was no sign of the girl, just the tattered remains of a white dress hanging from a willow tree on the bank. The girl's corpse was never found, which came as no surprise—the lake was deep; its murky depths hid many a broken body and shattered dream. But four weeks later the lord of the manor was discovered—face down in his own fountain. And by the time the first snow covered the ground like wedding lace, the hapless blacksmith's son was dead too. The doctor who examined his body refused to comment, but the villagers whispered that the young man's face was twisted with terror and that clenched tightly in his fist was a single green-leafed sprig of willow. But surely these were just rumours—after all, willows shed their leaves long before winter falls. . . .

WOLVERSHIEL
John Gaskin

Wolvershiel lies close in at the base of Ravens-
cleugh. In 1774, Robt. Robson of Wolvershiel
Hall was the owner. . . . Time and ruthless
hands have both dealt hardly with (it).

Dippie Dixon

Cold beneath dark skies, shards of rain splattering themselves on
dry ground and being swept away again by the wind, black
clouds scudding over hard land, comfortless twilight throughout
the long northern day—and the day June the third. I am
supposed to be on holiday. My wife has taken our daughter to
the Crimea to recover from her latest divorce. I had pushed off a
book to my publisher some weeks earlier and received a polite
rejection of the sort 'very readable but we are afraid it will not
fit in our stable'.

In a spasm of anger with everyone I swept a few things into a
bag and drove up here to get away from myself, and with the
excuse that I would have a look at a bit of country I thought I
remembered visiting with my mother when I was very small, and
to which we never returned. It is a shallow dish of land set into
the side of the hills where it conceals a house of curious shape.
The place is a mile or two from a minor road to the north that
wriggles up the far side of the valley and eventually leads over
the watershed to Redesdale. I seemed to remember something of

it. But after the events of two days ago I am no longer sure what I imagine and what is real.

I am staying with Josephene and Harry Fogin at their farm at Westerhope which has been adapted for bed and breakfast accommodation. It is very comfortable; and Mrs Fogin has been most kind while I prolong my stay to recover from the fall, and whatever else happened. I am writing this in her little-used parlour while normal family life carries on in the kitchen. It is the normality that is so reassuring, and the thoughtless greetings of the Border Collies, ever eager to help by pushing their noses into your hand and upsetting tea cups.

It was two days ago that I set out full of enthusiasm to walk to Wolvershiel. The weather was unseasonably dreary, but not as forbidding as it is now, and on a long walk a man finds himself, even when he has to admit to being of an age that ought to have found itself years ago.

I told the Fogins where I was going, and that I would end by walking across the valley to catch the late afternoon bus. Harry looked a bit thoughtful and said I would have to cross the ford above Thorpcot, and that I ought to be careful poking around Wolvershiel. 'Of what?' I asked him. He said that it was a ruinous place. There had been cellars beneath it belonging to an older building, and some years earlier—before his time—there was an accident of some sort. So it was fenced off in the interests of safety to keep stock and hikers from straying in. I promised to be careful.

I set out with a flask of sherry and a ham sandwich in my pocket, and the general feeling of well-being one experiences on shedding for a time one's own and other people's cares. The sky was grey, but no rain was forecast, and the walking was good. I had originally intended to follow the contour from Westerhope, but it felt more enterprising to climb up to Ravenscrag by the forestry roads and take the long descent from the north.

It was past one o'clock when I broke free from the dense conifers at a point where a tumbled stone dyke went straight down the hill in the general direction I wanted. I thought I could see the abandoned steadings of Wolvershiel, and the stock enclosure, but it was some distance below, and I did not know precisely where to look, or where I had emerged from the forest. It could have been the outline of some other farm.

It is odd how unhelpful even a detailed map can be if you don't already know the general lie of the land, or precisely where you are. The forestry had been established since mine had been surveyed, and I could find several indications of boundaries running more or less north-south, any one of which could have been the dyke I was looking at. On its right was scrubby wood-land; on the left rough, very rough, almost precipitous pasture. I slithered and stumbled down to where the land began to flatten out. Wind torn hedges of thorn and brambles replaced the broken walls, and I could no longer see what I had taken to be Wolvershiel, although it must have been more or less straight ahead, concealed in the shorter horizon.

I sat down to enjoy the sherry and sandwiches. It was not cold, but neither was it light—merely one of those shadowless days when even in high summer everything looks drab and featureless. The dry gorse in the hedge rustled with some unfelt movement of the air. The usual sounds of sheep and cattle were missing. The experience ought to have been depressing, but I was pleased with myself: well exercised, pleasantly refreshed, and with an easy walk ahead across the valley. I was also strangely elated and expectant. It was here, if anywhere, that I would feel again the reassurance of familiarity. But beyond the hedge was only another nondescript field, and beyond that another hedge, and these meant nothing to me. Ahead, the beginnings of a path gradually evolved into a rutted track confined on one side by a stony bank pitted with rabbit holes, and muffled by half dead bushes and withered grass.

It was as I walked past a partly exposed boulder that I experienced the flickering of familiarity that is usually called *déjà vu*. I would prefer to call it simply 'the already seen'. On closer inspection the already seen was not a boulder but a rough-hewn stone cut with a single step, almost certainly an old mounting-block. It lay abandoned on one side of the track trying to rekindle for me a familiarity that led nowhere. But for no reason I could identify the thing changed my mood from pleasant anticipation to a kind of empty, unfocused foreboding. I did not know if I had been there before, or if I had, whether for example it could have been before or after the death of the elder brother I had been too young to remember, and about whom nobody ever spoke. It was apparently one of those tragedies that are so painful that even to speak of them is to revive an experience of something dreadful. I always thought it must have been a fire, or some domestic accident for which my mother felt responsible. For some years I didn't even know I had had a brother, and by the time childhood ignorance had become adult curiosity she was dead, and my father's life has always been beyond the limits of memory.

However, none of these musings seemed remotely relevant to the mounting-block, and when I turned away I was at once diverted by the sight of Wolvershiel across a field. It looked as if there could have been two houses close together. The grey walls were half concealed by birch and alder, and a dark area, perhaps rampant nettles, obscured the ground close to the buildings. But it looked as if still roofed with the stone slabs common to old buildings in that area, and although the windows appeared to be no more than black holes in the masonry, there was no sign of general collapse. The place was really quite close and obvious, and I wondered how I had failed to see it earlier. The appearance was, however, not inviting, and I almost walked on leaving the ruin to its own devices. But, seeing it was the contrived excuse for my walking at all, and I would feel later as if I had cheated myself if I made no attempt to look closer. It would also give me something to talk about with the Fogins. Anyway, I was curious, and curiosity is difficult to resist, as a number of dead cats proverbially testify.

I left the path to cross an oddly triangular field that was fenced with the usual pig netting and barbed wire. At its far side a lane converged with another track that was obviously used for herding sheep, and by the ubiquitous quad bikes that modern farmers find indispensable and thieves irresistible. But at the point where I reached the lane a waist-high length of stone wall replaced the fence. I could see the buildings clearly, still with the forbidding foreground of dark growth that seemed to isolate the place from the surrounding country and threatened to make a direct approach impossible. Without thinking or looking properly I vaulted the wall.

For a fleeting instant that was strangely prolonged and slow I knew that the lane beyond was not where it should be. The wall was a kind of ha-ha, and the ground on its far side was a yard or more below the level of the field. I was in the wrong position in mid air and came down on my back. The blow was shattering, and I must have lost consciousness—for how long I cannot say, except that when I fell the sky was a light mottled grey. When I opened my eyes at the sound of a remote voice asking if I was all right, the sky was featureless and darker than it had been.

'Let me help you.'

Dark World

The arm was under my head and shoulders, and I was being lifted up and set on my feet; feet I did not quite own or feel.

My helper was a small, oldish man, with a bald or shaven head, who must have been much stronger than he looked to judge from the way he got me up. I did not seem able to focus clearly on his face, or for the moment on anything.

'Can you walk?' he asked, and then, without waiting for an answer, he continued, 'We must get you to the house. You'll need to lie down for a while in case there are any after effects. One can't be too careful with concussion. My wife will help. She has a lot of experience.'

It was only then that I saw he was not alone, and that on my other side stood a tall silent woman unseasonably draped in a long, flat, old-fashioned, belted mackintosh. I supposed, if I supposed anything, that the sky had been threatening rain when she and her husband left the house.

With one each side I walked—floated would be a better description—along a short drive to what now appeared to be two houses joined at ground level by a short, windowless passage or wall, the block on the right being an exact but smaller replica of the one on the left, the whole forming a symmetry like a dumb-bell with one end larger than the other. There was a central door in each building. I was led to the door on the right, the entrance to the smaller structure. As if sensing my confusion the woman said—

'This is the children's side. Those are their rooms. If any are ill, but not too ill, we put the bed in the middle so that they can share in the play of the others by watching it. We all do that here.'

I couldn't find the right words to ask if 'they' were her own children or if we were in an orphanage of some sort. But the place seemed too quiet for a children's home.

'They are happy,' she said, leaving me as ignorant as before.

What we had entered was a square atrium to which light was admitted by a central cupola. In the middle was a single bed, and I saw something moving restlessly on it in a way that made me wonder if the tenant was badly deformed in some way, but I was still too dazed to look closely. On the wall opposite the entrance and again on the right were symmetrically placed doors that must have been the children's rooms. All were closed. In the middle of the wall to the left a single dark archway without a door led, as I was shortly to be shown, to a larger mirror image of the room where we now stood.

'That's a little boy who fell and hurt his head near here just as you did. His mother's in the other wing. She'll know you but you can't see her yet. Come this way.'

She motioned towards the stone arch and a passageway beyond while I wondered how someone could know me without knowing who I was or seeing me first. At first I could only detect another arch ahead of us which turned out to be further away than it looked: then we were in a substantially larger version of the first room, except that in the middle, instead of a bed, and protected by a low stone balustrade, was what appeared to be a dark circle of water, somewhat akin to a cold northern representation of the fountain and pool in the atrium of a classical Greek or Roman villa.

'It's not water,' he said apologetically. The woman had contrived to disappear. 'We thought that would be too dangerous, and it might flood the lower rooms that we keep for the naughty ones, so we just painted the inside black to give the impression of water. It used to be the top of the old well.'

My head was beginning to ache abominably, and I was afraid I might be ill at any moment. Evidently he noticed my distress, and wafted me to a great sofa that was located against the far wall.

'Lie still for a while,' he said. 'We'll get help, but you won't need it. The children will not disturb you. We have them under control.'

I was incapable of resisting or of thinking very much, and I was becoming concerned that I had really done myself some damage—not to bone or muscle, but to my nervous system, for I had no feeling of anything; only sight of a sort, and hearing. I lay still at his bidding, alone in the silence, facing across the room towards the pond, the dark archway leading to the smaller house beyond it. Only then did I register what was peculiar about the arch. It was in proportion to the room I was now in, bigger than the one at the far end. The connecting passage had been designed like a funnel so that anyone coming from the small atrium to the larger would feel as if they were walking down a passage shorter than it was, and wider than they expected.

My mind must have wandered, but to a purpose, for I knew why the building was familiar. Years earlier I had been in a place like it, but there the units were round, not square. That was in Perthshire. I believe Knockshannoch was the name—an old hunting lodge. The smaller circular building housed the servants' quarters with a kitchen and stove in the centre. The larger one contained the guest rooms. Its central area served as common room and dining room. In the middle a huge fireplace had opened hospitably on four sides, not a dark pit of imitation water, and the stone chimney had soared up to the centre of the vaulted roof with all the confidence of a mighty column in a Norman cathedral.

The day-dream was reassuring, but I was drawn back to present things by a sound. Somewhere I could hear a voice that seemed to be speaking endearments that were not answered.

The voice was a woman's, and it stirred a remote sense of familiarity. It was not his wife. It must, I felt, be the mother of the little boy in the adjacent hall. The voice was gentle and comforting, like coming to a warm room and a loving family at the end of a journey undertaken long ago. But the sound was fading with the light, and I could no longer discern the whole room. Only the archway and the balustrade in the centre were clear, and now there was movement.

A vague shape hovered at the far end of the tunnel, and was coming closer. I almost laughed. It was a child in white pyjamas too big for him, playing blind-man's-buff, holding out his arms, stationary in the middle of the entrance, too far from the walls to find them. Then I saw it was not a game. He was alone. His head and eyes were bandaged, and there was blood on the bandages. After his fall the wounds must have been dressed in that thoughtless way, or perhaps the bandage had slipped down and he was too frightened to push it back. He took a step forward, hands groping about in empty air encountering nothing. In his darkness he must have got out of bed to feel for a door or wall that would guide him to his mother's voice. Instead of finding anything he had walked haplessly into the open tunnel, beyond the limits of the room, without touching the entrance, and on, impossibly far, lost into space without dimension, a void beyond meaning or natural terror.

At last the nightmare quality of his experience sank into my fuddled brain. I tried to get up to help him, but my limbs would not obey my will. Nothing connected between brain and body. It was like being turned to lead, or as a baby might feel rolled round with too many swaddling-clothes while his cot caught fire and burned around him. The physical paralysis was unbreakable. I tried to call out but could produce no sound. I could only see and experience his terror, and what I saw will be with me until I am unknowing dust.

He stumbled, and ran towards me crying, straight into the balustrade that surrounded the imaginary pond concealing the well. The stone edge caught him below the knee and his forward momentum threw him forward, over and down. His scream fell away into the abyss and there was silence. A door opened. From somewhere in the darkness came a cry of anguish in a voice I knew. The knowledge fragmented into a fire of memory and fear while something vast and insane soared up into the firmament above me. I grovelled beneath it, helpless because it was without understanding.

A muddy wellington boot was close to my face, and above it, in grotesquely foreshortened form, I was looking up at the leggings and heavy jacket of a man. He bent down, and I could hear the whirr of an idle engine close by; a quad bike, ordinary and unthreatening. I don't know what nonsense I blurted out at first, but it must have been enough to tell him I wasn't much good for comments about the weather or discussion of stock prices.

'Why man, lie still. You're in a bad way. What happened?'

I mumbled something about a well, but he heard something else.

'Yes, the wall's a real deceiver. You're not the first person who's fallen. Stay put. I'll have to get help. Ned's borrowed my mobile.'

But I did not want to let him go for reasons I could not properly convey.

'Let me see if anything's broken,' I croaked. 'I may be okay.'

'Take it easy then. Try one bit at a time.'

I had come to lying on my back. He helped me onto my side, and then into a kneeling position. My neck was stiff, my head hurt violently when I moved, and I felt sick, but nothing appeared to be broken, and upon trial everything seemed to be in working order after a fashion. When I stood up I nearly fell down again, but he caught me.

'You can't go on alone,' he declared. 'Can you sit on the bike behind me and hold on until we reach the road. It's not far. Then I'll get the van and run you home. Where are you staying?'

I told him Westerhope, the Fogin's place; which of course he knew, as all good farmers know other farms for miles around, especially when there are sheep involved.

He got me onto the bike and I held on as a squirrel holds on to a tree. Every bump sent a shriek of pain down my neck, but the journey was brief.

'Sit here,' he ordered. 'I'll be back with the Land Rover in a moment.'

He was about five minutes, during which time I managed to claw together some of the distraught fragments of my experience. I had seen it before. My brother climbing the mounting-block, tripping, and falling on his face. Our mother taking us to the nearest dwelling for help. The rest—the rest I could not have seen. I was with her. But I had heard. And now I wish I did not remember.

The Fogins have been most kind, and Dr Bell has visited every day in the old fashioned way that most doctors now avoid. There are bruises, and a bit of a problem with my neck, but nothing that rest and care will not cure. Except that I set out to hunt memories; now I am hunted by them. I have not sought additional information about Wolvershiel. Part of me does not want to know, but Harry Fogin, knowing where I had the accident, insisted upon talking about the place. Had I found it?

I said yes. I'd been quite close to it when I fell over the wall. It was a queer-looking double house. He gave me an odd look and said I couldn't have seen much.

'Apart from holes in the ground, a roofless barn, and the fenced-off well, there's nothing there now,' he said. 'Brown the builder took most of the stone for one of his housing schemes years ago.'

'But . . .' I began, and just managed to stifle the question in time. I did not want to give him the impression that I was delusional, or had found the wrong place, or worse, that I had been under the influence of drugs of some kind. Unfortunately curiosity had been aroused. 'So what became of the last owners?' I asked casually.

'They weren't owners—not even locals. Only been in the county thirty years or so they say. They were tenants of the Robsons. Fancied they ran the place as a foster home. Loonies. According to my Dad there were never any children there, bar one, and he died. They went to live—well sort of live—in a "home" near Oxford. The Warnford. I remember the name because there's a Warrenford up above Beaucastle.'

'But why was the house abandoned? I would have thought a place like that would be quite valuable these days.'

'Well it wasn't these days then, and there was a dispute about access. Some said this and others claimed that, and no one wanted to live there. So it went away to ruin. You could probably dig up the whole story in old copies of the *Gazette* if you're curious.'

Yes, I probably could, but nothing good can come if it, and I must remember the fate of certain dead cats.

THE ARNDALE PASS
Corinna Underwood

In the deepest shadows, furthest from the candle's dance, there is safety. This is where I sit, where she cannot find me. Her strange being cannot reach beyond the rim of brightness; the blink of a solitary candle is enough to contain her. Only in the power of brighter illumination can she approach clarity.

It was in the morning's sunlight shafts sloping through the windows that I first saw her again. Drawn together in languid dust motes, her slim form stood there, watching me walk down the hallway. Between the two breaths I took on seeing her, enough time passed to take my life away. She was smiling almost, and I was reminded again of the last time I had seen her face; frozen in a contortion of disbelief and horror as she fell away.

We bought this house because it is light and airy but now it has too many windows—but I have learned the efficacy of heavy drapes. She can no longer follow me from room to room, vanishing in the gloom only to reappear in the mid-morning halos. It began as my morning ritual to traipse through the house pulling the thick curtains closed before daylight crept in. Now I do not bother to open them, even at night. The full moon can be enough to tempt her from the shadows of death to watch me with her mocking grimace.

I have reinvented myself to suit the night, sleeping while the sun shines and rising only at sunset to begin working on my manuscripts. Sometimes I catch myself listening as though I might hear the rustle of her skirt, the click of her heels or that final, silent scream.

There is always the falling. If I blink my eyes too slowly it is there, and in my dreamloop of the fatal few seconds I begin to ask myself why I could not hold on. There is no answer either in her silent scream or her mocking sneer.

It is morning. The sun is stabbing bright needles through a crack in the drapes and for a moment she is there and I cannot bring myself to rush forwards to blot out her traces. She stands hands on hips, as she often did to chide me, that taunting stare stretching her hard face into an ugly mimic of a smile. I gulp some air and rush to set the drapes close and for a split second before blackness resumes I hear it.

I cannot leave the house. Where would I go? Perhaps on one of our favourite walks, perhaps the last one? Getting out of the house, the doctor said, would do me good. I could retrace my steps perhaps, and walk the Arndale Pass; awkward to navigate even in the best conditions. It is such a steep path, falling away at random intervals. It is said that many lovers have made a pact and jumped to their demise there. This is the kind of story that she loved; drama to excess. She called it passion and said that without it she could not live.

It was on our first trip to the Arndale Pass that her obsession had begun. How many lovers had jumped there? How many loving souls had become entwined for all eternity? How strong would one's love need to be to make such a pact? Her speculations became wilder and wilder and I became more and more anxious. I should have seen where she was heading.

Why did I agree to go there that day? I had already decided that it was over.

I was being cowardly; struggling for the right words to tell her, but I convinced myself it was just for old time's sake. All along the pass she told me how much she loved me, how fate had brought us together and how we would always be, in this life and the hereafter. She said she would rather die than be without me. She really shouldn't have said that. Until then, I hadn't considered it an option. I had let her hold my hand just one last time. The path was slick from the rain, I barely nudged her. It was so easy to let go.

There is a knock at the door. It is my grocery delivery. Usually I don't answer. Eventually he will leave it on the door step where I can retrieve it after dark, but today it's raining and I don't want it to get wet. As soon as I open the door she is there, smirking at me as though she knows some dreadful secret. The box of groceries is heavy and in my haste to return to the safety of my shadows I slip on the door step. Everything after happens in slow motion. I drift through the air. A jar of peanut butter smashes on the lower step. I am a contortionist. My left arm is first to reach the ground, my right leg follows, then the back of my neck. I am surprised that there is no pain. The last thing I see is her smile of triumph as I fall away.

ORACLE
Rosalie Parker

I was pretty angry when I first came to Coverdale, but I suppose that's not altogether surprising. Most of the world was angry in 1940.

My parents had decided that I'd be better off in North Yorkshire than Sheffield, where we lived in a leafy suburb called Kenwood. Their decision, the reason for which was ostensibly to spirit me away from the imminent bombing of the city, might also have had something to do with the fact that my mother had left the family home to move in with her 'friend' Mr Vickers. My father, an obstetric surgeon, was finding it hard to recruit a reliable person to look after me in the school holidays while he worked his interminable shifts at the hospital.

I don't know if it is possible to die of shame, but in those first months of my parents' separation my father looked as if he might. The 1940s were a different world—what the neighbours thought was a kind of life or death. My father was a proud man, usually fair, but he believed implicitly in the values of conventional life, and something in him was mortally injured by my mother's desertion. He went about with a closed face, as if he hoped he was invisible.

My parents' arguments had been a constant factor throughout my childhood, punctuated by increasingly infrequent periods of glum reconciliation. I think they loved each other, but they were incompatible, she having much more spirit than him. I hadn't seen my mother very often in the weeks following her departure, but she seemed happy, happier than she had ever been with us.

I liked my day-school, and I had two very good friends, Stephen and James, who lived nearby and with whom I often played. So I was extremely unimpressed, to say the least, when, at the beginning of August I was told that I was to stay for the foreseeable future with my father's cousin Millie. Aunt Millie lived in an obscure village some 100 miles north in the Yorkshire Dales, and was married to an army captain, a professional soldier in the Yorkshire Regiment. She was much involved with the local Women's Voluntary Service and probably only agreed to have me because my father was able to pay her a generous allowance.

For the first time in my young life I argued with my father. He seemed genuinely astonished that I should question his will. His face grew strained and white.

'I have discussed it with your mother, Martin, and she agrees with me. You will be better off in the country with Aunt Millie. You're only ten and we—I—am responsible for your welfare. I think I can still be relied upon to know what's best for you. Now let that be an end to it.'

I lost my temper—reason and restraint fled.

'You know nothing about me! You don't love me! You're only thinking of yourself! . . . No wonder mummy left! . . .'

I ran upstairs to my bedroom, slamming the door behind me so hard that the windows rattled. It took me some time to calm down, and when the anger left me, as it did all of a sudden, I felt deflated and sick with misery and resentment. When I put my ear to the door, all was silent. Throughout the evening, Father did not come. I finally put myself to bed and passed an uncomfortable, feverish night. The next morning, hunger and thirst drove me downstairs.

Father was already sitting at the breakfast table. He looked tired.

'Please try to make the best of things, Martin. It will be easier for you.'

I merely took some toast and marmalade and chewed on it in silence.

My father, by today's standards, was a very reticent man. I have recently come to realise that I have turned out very much like him.

୫୨

We hardly exchanged a word until the next Saturday morning when my small blue suitcase, until then used only for our annual summer holidays in the West Country, was packed, and my father drove me in his new green Humber up into the hill country of the Northern Dales. It was a very hot summer and the car was stifling. For some reason of his own my father insisted on driving with the windows closed. The heat shimmered off the road and the desiccated grass on the verges.

We had not visited Aunt Millie since I was a baby. I had often half-listened to my mother and father discussing her and Uncle Simon at the dinner table. I dimly recalled that my father disapproved of the fact that Aunt Millie had no children, and my mother that Uncle Simon was so often absent. Because of the War, his visits home were likely to be even less frequent. I knew also that they lived in a village that my mother had referred to on more than one occasion as 'godforsaken'.

During our journey, which took far longer than I expected, (after we had reached Skipton the roads became increasingly narrow and tortuous), my father began talking about the War.

'I am going to treat you as a grown-up, Martin. As you know, our Spitfires and Hurricanes are shooting at German aeroplanes in an attempt to keep this country free. No-one knows what the outcome will be. Some people think that Hitler will invade within weeks. Days, even. I am doing what I think is best in making sure that you are safe.'

It was a big speech for him. I sulked furiously and silently beside him.

'When you have grown up, and I intend that you shall, I think you will understand me a little better than you are allowing yourself to now.'

I'm afraid I was relentless, and merely stared out of the passenger seat window. As we passed through Kettlewell and headed up the steep pass into Coverdale, I let my dark mood colour my perception, and saw the astonishing landscape as only incalculably barren and bleak.

The road that led into the dale was practically impassable, and it seemed to me that we were heading away from all that was civilised and worthwhile. I could see nothing but grass, sheep and moorland, and the occasional stone-built house or barn. The very few settlements we passed through were tiny and deserted. My father had grown silent, and as we drove around a right hand bend into Carlton, it seemed that there was an unbridgeable gulf between us.

The village where Aunt Millie lived straggles along the road for almost a mile, and is by far the most populous settlement in Coverdale—which in all honesty isn't saying very much. The stone houses huddle together against the Dales weather and were built mainly, I later discovered, in the eighteenth and nineteenth centuries during a boom in the wool trade. Aunt Millie's house, Clovelly Dene, was a tall, double-fronted Georgian house with clipped yew hedges growing in the small front garden and up against the house. My father, gripping the handle of my suitcase, steered me up the short path and rapped loudly on the front door. Despite my misery, I noticed that the door-knocker took the form of a finely-detailed brass fox's head. It was only one of many curios and antique knick-knacks that I was to discover Aunt Millie had about the house.

℘

My father did not stay long, and when he had left (and I'm afraid I gave him only a cursory 'goodbye Father' at our parting), Aunt Millie, best described as tall and no-nonsense, showed me my room.

'It's serviceable,' she said. 'I hope it will do. You can light the fire whenever you like, but you're responsible for cleaning out the ashes and resetting it. It's probably a bit warm for a fire at the moment, but from September the evenings will be chilly. We have the same climate here as the Highlands of Scotland.'

In fact it was a beautifully proportioned room, having the tall ceiling of all the rooms in the house, an array of intriguing inbuilt cupboards and a large original fireplace. There was newspaper and kindling in the grate, and a stack of firewood and a bucket of coal already in place beside it. On the mantelpiece was a selection of novelty Victorian vesta cases, some made of silver, in the shape of animals, each one of which I soon came to know intimately. An oil lamp stood on the bedside cabinet. It seemed electricity had yet to reach Coverdale.

I managed a desultory 'it's fine,' and pretended not to notice that Aunt Millie gave me a rather searching look.

'I expect it will take you a little while to settle in, old chap. I won't be around much in the daytime, so you can suit yourself. Have a good explore. Just don't rub any of the farmers up the wrong way. They all carry shotguns around here.' She laughed her hearty laugh, and I couldn't tell if she was serious or not.

We got along together perfectly well for the next few days, me not saying much, she making the kind of inane conversation she thought a ten-year-old boy might like to hear. Despite my continued resentment, I became intrigued by her collection of curios. There were candlesticks on every surface, of porcelain, brass and silver. She also had some Japanese woodblock prints hanging on the walls, depicting the Kabuki actors and famous geishas of the Floating World. They seemed to me a little like the cartoon characters in some of my favourite comics. Everywhere you turned there was something surprising and novel. Eventually my fascination got the better of me and I plucked up the courage to ask Aunt Millie about them.

'Oh, I have to keep myself occupied while Uncle Simon is away. As he's *usually* away, I've acquired a sizeable assortment of treasures! I haunt the local junk shops and auction rooms, and before the War I sometimes took the train to Newcastle or London, to see what I could find. Uncle Simon thinks I'm quite potty, of course.'

She was busy with her voluntary War work for most of the daytime and early evenings. After the first couple of days of my stay, which I spent sulking and reading *Great Expectations*, found in the bookcase in my room, I began to venture out into the village. Apart from our holidays in Devon or Cornwall, which had been spent mainly at the seaside, I knew little about the country, and cared less.

The village still basked in what seemed like a never-ending blaze of sunshine. I discovered that there were some amenities— Brown's motor repair garage, a cheerful-looking public house called The Foresters' Arms, a small grocers' store and a butchers' shop. A group of local children stared at me as I strolled past the stolidly-built Victorian church and school. I poked my tongue out at them and they scuttled away.

The scenery was of course stunning, but Sheffield is a hilly, surprisingly green city, and I could at first find nothing to admire in my new surroundings. Everything seemed mean and small and alien, and there was very little that I could find to do.

I could see that the fell-tops above the houses were clothed in purple, and when I asked Aunt Millie about it, she told me that it was the time of year when the heather was in bloom.

'Why don't you walk up on the moor and have a look? Stick to the paths and you'll be fine. You might see some grouse.'

Pride prevented me from admitting to her that I didn't feel confident enough to venture that far into unknown territory. Instead, one afternoon in my second week in Carlton, feeling thoroughly disgruntled and out of sorts, I walked down to the river, the Cover, which ran along the bottom of the V-shaped valley. As I followed the grassy path across the fields, curlew warbled their mournful cries above me. I was startled by a long-legged hare which bolted from a tuft of rough grass and hurtled off into the centre of the field.

When I reached the river I found that, as a result of the hot dry weather, it was very low. The narrow stream of water was coloured brown by the peat from the moors above. After staring into the stream for some time I spotted some fish skilfully maintaining their position under a cloud of midges—three or four fat speckled trout.

I walked eastwards along the southern bank of the river, reasoning that I would not lose my way if I stuck close to the water. After half a mile or so I saw, on the northern side, a ruined stone building. I remembered that Aunt Millie had told me about it. It was called St Simon's Chapel. In earlier centuries it had been a chapel-of-ease conveniently situated between

Carlton and the villages on the other side of the dale. At one point it had even been converted into a tavern, providing another kind of comfort to the hard working farmers of Coverdale. I crossed the decaying wooden bridge and could see that it was abandoned and roofless, overgrown with moss and bracken. I picked up a stick and poked around the surrounding nettles and saplings. The river bank here was deep in the shade of tall ash trees. Although it was still the middle of the day it was gloomy, quiet and still, except for the swish, swish of my stick, and the faint tinkle of the river as it flowed over the shallow bed of cobbles.

It must have crept up on me gradually, but I became aware of a sort of faint, high, melodic sound. I stood still so that I could listen more carefully. It was a female voice, singing something pleasing and tuneful that I did not recognise. The singing seemed to come from inside the chapel ruins, and as I tiptoed towards them, intent now on making as little noise as possible, it gradually increased in volume.

I made my way warily into the ruins, and there stood a woman—a youngish woman, although I was no judge then. I think now that she must have been around thirty-five, the same sort of age as my mother. Her thick brown hair was arranged on top of her head and she wore a long, light dress that flowed from under her bust. She looked like a character on a Greek vase. In her left hand she grasped some green foliage. She was singing her song and appeared to be staring straight at me.

She stopped singing and smiled. It is impossible to describe the beauty of her smile. When she spoke, it was with a faintly foreign lilt that I could not place, but her voice was charming.

'Hello, Martin. I hope you are well today?'

Puzzled that she knew my name, and unsure how to respond, English good manners took over.

'I'm very well, thank you.'

She smiled again. A wave of well-being washed over me.

'That is good. Do you know, I think today *is* a good day, because you have come to see me. Move closer, Martin.'

I shuffled towards her.

'I see that you are quite a big boy now. Quite a clever boy, too, I think.'

'It's kind of you to say so.'

'And polite, too! What a joy! Soon you will be a man, Martin, making your own way in the world. What will you be? What do you *want* to be?

'I don't know. Maybe a pilot, or the captain of a ship. Or a pirate.'

'I see you have the spark of adventure in you.'

'I'd like to travel a long way away from here.'

'Travel is good . . . home is best. But where is your home? Where are the people that you care for? You must not be afraid to show your love, and be strong. Life is not always roses, or toys and books and sweets. You must be strong for your mother's and father's sake.'

I couldn't understand why she was spoiling what had been an intriguing conversation about me by bringing my parents into it.

'Why should I care about *them*? They don't love *me*.'

'You think not? I see you still have some growing up to do. It seems you will have to learn the hard way what caring for someone else really means.'

The old fury overtook me.

'You don't know what you're talking about! It's all rubbish.'

She sighed.

'If only that were true.'

It had grown almost as dark as twilight. I realised with a start of horror that her stare was still unbroken. Her eyes were fixed. She could not blink.

'Know thyself, Martin. Life is not a painting, beautiful and the same for all time. You will survive, and change, and grow. And live. You must go now.'

'Okay,' I said ungraciously.

A rook started up from one of the ash trees and flapped off towards the fields. I stalked out of the building without looking back.

∾

I did not know what to make of the odd encounter, so, as children do, I put it to the back of my mind and all but forgot it.

I walked the mile or so back to Carlton. Nearer the village, the path ran past the large walled garden of a white-painted house, and the drowsy drone of bees gorging on the flowering plants and bushes followed me up the slight incline onto the village road. When Aunt Millie returned, she took one look at me shivering and dozing in the chair, and sent me straight to bed. I was fine the next morning.

After that first exploration I began to walk further afield, over to the village of West Scrafton on the other side of the dale, and then finally up on to Melmerby Moor, the moor above Carlton. I climbed Penhill, and found that I could see as far north east as the Cleveland Hills and the steelworks of Middlesborough. A sharp pang of homesickness clawed at my guts as I spotted smoke rising from the factories and furnaces.

Over the weeks I explored as far as I could walk. I met few people on my adventures, and I did not seek them out. I still felt raw and savage, but gradually I found that the hurt and disappointment in my father was fading away. In short, I discovered a renewed interest in life.

Aunt Millie took me on some of her antiquing expeditions, which I enjoyed much more than I expected to. She had a real interest and expertise in the social history of small objects of desire, and I found her enthusiasm infectious.

I devoured the books I found in Aunt Millie's bookcases. While listening to the wireless in the evenings she watched with some amusement as I sat in her comfortable sitting room, reading about hallmarked silver, Chinese porcelain, wild flowers and birds, English country furniture.

'We'll make a countryman of you yet, Martin. Or an antique dealer.'

As August rolled into September, and then the bitterly cold winter of 1940-41, I settled into life in Coverdale. I was never bored—there was always a new walk or a thrilling new book to explore—and I began to help Aunt Millie with the business of running the house. She did not believe in keeping a maid from the War effort, so I carried coal and chopped wood, shopped for provisions and scrubbed the stone flags of the kitchen floor. I even learned to cook. From time to time my father wrote me letters—short, impersonal scrawls about his work. I did not bother to reply.

A foot or two of snow covered the village in January, and life became harder. Food and petrol rationing took a firm hold, and I came to appreciate the hardiness and resourcefulness of the villagers. I made some friends, firstly among the shopkeepers and tradesmen I had dealings with, and then more generally. Aunt Millie, although an outsider, was well liked, and when people found out I was her sort-of nephew, I was accepted without having to try very hard to impress.

Oracle

Spring in Coverdale was late but memorable. The curlew returned in March, and soon the pale yellow primroses punctuated the grassy banks and verges. By May there was a real warmth to the sun. School had not been mentioned, and I had no intention of reminding anyone. I continued to roam the countryside and happily read all the books I could lay my hands on.

One day in early June, Aunt Millie announced that Uncle Simon would soon be coming home on leave. We decided that we would push the boat out and make the house especially jolly and welcoming. Aunt Millie gave me some money so that I could scout around for a few extra supplies. Many local farmers' wives kept chickens, and I knew that I should be able to buy eggs and maybe even butter and meat.

The day before Uncle Simon was due, while we were arranging a vase of roses picked from the garden, the telegram boy knocked at the door. Aunt Millie returned to the sitting room holding the thin, folded paper as if it were some kind of poison. She sat down heavily. I felt dreadfully sorry for her.

'Would you like me to open it for you, Aunt Millie?'

'No, no. Bless you, Martin. It must be borne, I suppose.'

I watched as she read the short message. I was already beginning to think of ways to try to make her happy again.

Her face crumpled, and she clutched the chintz material of the chair.

'Is Uncle Simon . . . ?'

'Yes . . . well . . . Martin. . . . The telegram says that he has been killed. . . . I mean, your father has been killed. He was working in a hospital in Birmingham when there was an air raid. He carried on with the operation until the baby was safely delivered and the mother attended to. Only then did he go to the shelter. There was a direct hit and he was killed instantly.

111

Twenty-four other people died. I'm sorry. I know that you cared for him very deeply.'

As I stood up, I knocked the vase of roses off the table. It smashed to pieces, the delicate red petals crushed on the floor.

ஐ

I stayed in Coverdale for another two weeks—they are rather hazy in my memory—and then my mother and her friend Mr Vickers came to collect me. Mr Vickers—Michael—eventually became my stepfather, and I lived with them quite happily in Sheffield, going back to my old school and doing well there. My friends James and Stephen accepted me back as if I had never been away. There were few serious bombing raids on the city.

My mother, who was a kind woman, spoke to me often about my father, telling me little things about him—how they met, and what a clever, well-respected doctor he was. She would have liked me to have trained as a surgeon, but it was not to be.

I followed up my interest in antiques and made a living, after a few years dealing in English silver, as an auctioneer. I moved to Cardiff and set up my own auction house, Coverdale's, which has been very successful. I have my dear wife and children, and I am in many ways a lucky man.

I have never been back to Carlton, but Aunt Millie wrote me wonderful letters right up until her death. Uncle Simon survived the War and they had a son and daughter, rather late in life. Once, not long after the War had ended, I wrote and asked Aunt Millie if she had ever heard of a blind woman, perhaps foreign, living nearby. She replied, without questioning why I had asked, that she had not.

THE HOUSE ON NORTH
CONGRESS STREET
Jason A. Wyckoff

If you are afforded the discretion of choosing *when* to spend a
terrifying night in a haunted house, I strongly recommend
opting for it during your college years. I doubt I could tolerate
the experience these twenty years later; certainly I could not
behave as resiliently as I did at the time. My psyche was
undoubtedly more pliable then, so much so that my experience,
though never forgotten, was quickly attenuated by more
pressing matters (here I wish I was speaking of academia, but as
with many other young men, my primary concern was the oft-
agonising pursuit of the fairer sex). It may be that my estimation
of life appraised such occurrences as more common than I have
since learned them to be. Possibly, I was more self-centred and
expected the exceptional to be routine for me. I feel there must
have been *something* special about me; I say this because I saw
the ghost, whereas my companions, one resident and one
frequent guest, did not, that night or any other. I believe I might
have been what is referred to as a 'sensitive'—whether or not I
remain so to this day I cannot ascertain. I have recognised no
other encounters with the supernatural.

It happened one year that I, a student at the Ohio State
University in Columbus, and my good friend Hayes, a student at
Ohio University in Athens, were both romantically involved
with co-eds attending Ivy League universities. As each school's

respective week-long 'spring break' coincided, we elected to take a road-trip to visit our paramours. We would be accompanied by a friend of Hayes's, Steve, who had nothing better to do and who was the only one among the three of us to own a car. As a spiteful aside, I might point out that the 'spring break' occurred in the middle of March, and the equinox marked its conclusion rather than its commencement. Regardless: I was retrieved from Columbus and taken back to Steve's house on North Congress Street (I'll leave off the exact number), where we three would spend the night before embarking on the next day's long drive. We prepared for departure with the customary discipline of three young men confident of their invulnerability. So let that be the first arrow in the sceptic's quiver: Yes, we imbibed enthusiastically. It will probably not serve my defence to mention that in this at least we were well studied. I remember how, impecunious as we were, we thought we would be thrifty by chipping in to buy a carton of cigarettes together, with the expectation it would last through the trip. I am not certain it lasted through to Providence.

Athens is a college town in southeastern Ohio, tucked amongst forested, swelling hills. Busy by day on campus and downtown in a saddle traced by the Hocking River, out from its centre the town reaches residential wings of increasing languorousness. When school is not in session, the town is strikingly quiet. One imagines it disappearing if the students forget to return. Sometime following my experience there, I heard that Athens is the thirteenth 'most haunted' town in the United States. I suppose if you can't be first in that category, then you might as well be thirteenth—I doubt Athens is the only town to have that claim made for her. The house on North Congress was unremarkable, a quaint American two-storey house with peaked roof, pale siding and dark trim (I remember it as white and blue). Approached from the street, it looked as likely owned by a grandmother as rented to a handful of students.

From a shallow porch the front door opened into the living room. The door was situated in the middle of the house, but because of a dividing wall to the left as one entered, the space opened to the right. A long, wide hallway ran the length of the house to the back door. Some modification had been made to accommodate the expected inhabitants; an opening to the left led to two bedrooms on the first floor that likely had been intended as a dining room and study. The base of a stairway sat along the right wall of the living room, catty-corner to the front door. A landing at the top of the stair opened onto two more bedrooms; turning right and taking a few steps back along the length of the stair led you to a large bathroom. Returning to the first floor: the hallway (passing a small alcove under the stairs) led to an open kitchen on the right and a small utility room on the left. This room had been converted to a recording studio. It was not large enough to accommodate much more than lo-fi sonic experimentation and solo recording. The room was bleak, poorly lit, and crowded over with an ivy of black patch cords and speaker wire immobilising two folding chairs and connecting a Frankensteinian collage of electrical equipment stacked atop tables, crates, and amplifiers. This room they called the Dungeon, variously because it was bitterly cold in winter and clammy in summer, because the walls and floor were bare and suffered from neglect, or arising from the claustrophobic conditions consequent of its purpose. But beyond those concerns, I was told the room was considered 'oppressive' or 'heavy'—and this impression was attributed to something more than the physical attributes of the space.

Dark World

And so I was initiated into the deeper mysteries of the house. Both Steve and Hayes claimed that the house was haunted, based both on their experiences as well as those of the other inhabitants. (Perhaps here I should point out that we three were alone in the house that evening, the other housemates having already departed. Alone, I should say, except for Steve's golden retriever, Rollo, who will feature prominently in the narrative.) As is the habit of young men, the matter was addressed with as much affected indifference as earnestness. While both claimed the appellation 'haunted' was the consensus opinion of all familiar with the property, likewise did they refrain from expressing any sense of wonder about its unusual status. That blasé repression impressed me initially as an attempt not to laugh—as though they were curious how far they could carry the ruse and were afraid if they oversold the concept, they wouldn't be able to constrain their mirth. So I listened dubiously, aware that I was the perfect target for such a joke, believer that I wanted to be. In addition to the 'heavy' atmosphere/presence often felt in the Dungeon, they testified that electrical devices in that room would switch on and off extemporaneously, and that objects of all sorts would be found throughout the house other than where they were left. These claims are easily refutable as claustrophobia, excessive cross-wiring, and living in a house populated by college students. I was surprised they offered no more grandiose claims, reporting neither inexplicable sounds or disembodied voices, nor sightings of apparitions or moving shadows. Any of those phenomena would fall within the realm of expectation for a truly 'active' haunted house. I did not pry beyond what was offered, but I believe I presented a willing audience if either cared to say more. Their reticence added validity to the claim; though guilt for pranking a friend would not hold them back (even if, as I said,

116

the artfulness of the ploy might benefit from it), embarrassment might. The overriding attitude of that age might be summed up as 'laboured cool'. Such studied nonchalance easily accommodates all manner of outlandish behaviour, but struggles to find the right reaction to the 'mundanely odd'. Of course, the subject of the supernatural is easily distrusted at any age. One is as wary of discomforting a friend or inviting ridicule from an unbeliever as one is of engaging someone whose enthusiasm for the subject greatly exceeds his own (and thereby eliciting worry that he might appear similarly overzealous to others).

I've noticed that, perhaps contrary to expectation, the more uncommon a conversational topic, the more devotion it requires from the participants to hold focus. Failing to engender the requisite enthusiasm, the subject of the haunting was dropped. No invitation to revisit it was offered, and I could not hope to make any mention of it that would be anything but awkward. Instead, we drank and smoked and talked of women measuredly and of music wantonly. We may have attempted some impromptu noise-making ourselves; I don't remember it, but it would have been par for the course. I remember Hayes was excited about the new Six Finger Satellite record, and we played it repeatedly. All other particulars are lost to time.

Eventually we called it a night. I must have shown at least some restraint that evening or I would have no story to tell. It is possible Hayes and Steve took a more direct route to unconsciousness. We all slept downstairs. Steve's room was at the front of the house; Hayes appropriated the vacant bedroom towards the back of the house. I laid down on a couch in the living room against the dividing wall. My head was towards the front door, my feet pointed down the hallway to the kitchen and the Dungeon. The couch was low and narrow; with my head on a pillow, I could see over the edge to the floor. The doors to the two bedrooms were left open. I know this because I checked, curious to see if Rollo had been shut out of Steve's bedroom. Judging by the indulgent affection Steve demonstrated for his dog, I imagined it likely that Rollo slept most nights on his master's bed. So I had thought it odd he lay down in front of the couch instead. Rollo did not attempt to share the couch with me. Neither did he sprawl on his side where I might reach out to scratch his head. Instead, he squatted Sphinx-like, facing towards the back of the house. After a time, he lowered his head on his paws but did not otherwise change position. He looked every bit the sentinel.

Just as I began to drift off, I heard the agitated murmur of a canine growl. Rollo's head remained flat, but his ears were perked forward. I looked down the hall toward the lighted kitchen but saw nothing. Rollo was silent for another minute. I closed my eyes. Rollo growled again, slightly louder. I looked and again saw nothing, but even as I stared in the same direction, still oblivious to the offence, Rollo growled again, louder.

I'm not too ashamed to say that I was becoming anxious. Perhaps just to hear my own voice, to hear any human voice. I mumbled, 'S'allright, Rollo. There, there.'

Silence again prevailed for another minute. Then Rollo growled again, a full-throated rumble; still I saw nothing. Rollo raised his head. He huffed twice, whistling through his teeth. I had no doubt he saw something I could not. Cold air met sweat on my temple. With the instinct of childhood I pulled my blanket over my ears and drew my feet up from the end of the couch. And in this position I watched Rollo, growling his warning, as he slowly, deliberately *turned his head*, watching some invisible presence as it crossed from the hall to the stairs. The interpretation of the action was unmistakable. I was as amazed as I was afraid. Rollo ticked his head sideways—one imagines the presence continued up to the second floor. The growling diminished, and then ceased. Rollo again lowered his head to his paws.

Rollo's agitation may have ebbed, but mine did not. Rationally, I knew very little had happened. An unhappy dog had moved its head; nothing else had I witnessed. Yet a palpable feeling of *intrusion* had passed through the room as the event occurred. Some might point out I was reacting to a suggestion imparted earlier in the day. The criticism is reasonable. I can argue only that this was one situation where removed impartiality fails—I am unfamiliar with any commonly accepted graduated measure of 'eerie'.

How long I lay there curled, tucked, and psychically shaken, I can't say, but the astute reader will have already anticipated my impending crisis. Did I not mention we were drinking copiously? I needed to relieve myself. And, as I have mentioned, the single bathroom in the house was upstairs. I considered urinating outside, but thought it likely that the opening of the front door (and the screen door beyond) would wake someone. There was less likelihood of that if I went out the back of the house, but it would require walking past the Dungeon, which I had been led to believe was the source of the disturbance, even if my own experience supposed the offender to have moved from the area. If I had been discovered utilising either exit, I would have been embarrassed. It would have been hardly unusual for a drunken young man to avail himself of nature, but it clearly made no sense to do so in that situation, as it required more effort than the expected course. Neither would I be able to explain myself: even if I was believed, fear is not easily empathised. I myself thought my disinclination to go upstairs was unnecessarily cautious. There was nothing for it but to use the proper facilities.

Dark World

I let my blanket fall away and shivered as the March evening air met my damp neck and scalp. When I rose from the couch, Rollo stood up. He looked at me expectantly—and possibly disappointedly, too, sensing that I failed to see what he saw, just as his master did. As I started towards the stairs, he crossed in front of me much as a seeing-eye dog might check his master when he approached an intersection. I bent and patted Rollo. He moved aside. I was encouraged by his lack of effort, thinking that though he may not much like the supposed spectral presence, neither was he overly concerned about it.

The wooden stairs creaked, of course. I was somewhat surprised to see one of the upstairs bedroom doors ajar. I would have expected anyone inhabiting a shared house to shut his door before leaving his room for a week. I took care not to stare too hard into the dark.

Jarringly bright fluorescent light sputtered to life from a naked tube mounted on one wall of the bathroom. I shut the door firmly. The commode was situated in the far corner next to a full-size tub (with opaque shower curtain drawn completely closed, of course, to conceal anything that might want to lie in wait). I can only blame the disagreeable light for making it seem terribly far away somehow. I had to cross in front of a mirror over the sink on the way. The drawn, red-eyed face I saw in it looked unnaturally wan, but it was at least familiar. As might be expected, my subsequent relief was profound. The affair completed, I washed up, opened the door, and turned off the light.

I noticed some slight movement. I did not see what moved, but I felt sure that the open bedroom door was now *more* open. Again, an explanation was readily available: the opening of one door occasioned a change in the air pressure that caused the other to swing. But it seemed as though I saw *less* dark than when I stepped into the hall—as though a shadow blocking part of the white door had disappeared into the room.

I hurried downstairs and thought no more of it. The End.

No, of course not. As disinclined as I had been to go upstairs in the first place, to the point of weighing unreasonable alternatives, I now felt driven to close the mystery. Perhaps my body, greedy for sleep, spurred my curiosity so that I might assuage my fear and thereby enable peaceful shutdown.

I considered and rejected two possibilities: one, that I had been misinformed about the departure of all the other housemates—this seemed preposterous, that Steve would either be wrong in his tally or that he would lie about it, and that someone had remained upstairs and unannounced; and two, that he or Hayes had changed bedrooms in the middle of the night—also unlikely, as I should have heard someone ascend the squeaky stairs, and likewise I doubted either of my inebriated companions could rush into an unfamiliar and darkened room stealthily.

I pushed the door open wide and felt along the wall for the switch. The light revealed the room vacant as reported. But I saw a section of blanket drooping from the empty single bed flutter near the floor. The furnace had kicked on with a hearty 'harrumph' when I was in the bathroom, but I did not think air escaping from a vent near the baseboard on the far side of the room could cause the movement. Here was another opportunity to defer, but I did instead what anyone denying his instincts would and pressed my stomach to the floor. I had seen the blanket move towards the top of the bed; I approached from the foot. I remember that I did not hesitate. I cannot say why I did not. I lifted the blanket and looked under the bed.

Because the blanket fell near to floor, little light ventured underneath, and the clutter of clothes, magazines, and unidentified paraphernalia was fuzzy with shadow. I was about to leave, very nearly disappointed for some ungodly reason, when I saw quite clearly towards the top of the bed the coiled figure of a boy. He stared at me from beneath a tangle of dark hair. I believe I read fear in his expression. I can only imagine what he saw in mine. My every nerve buzzed. I was more than simply afraid, though I was that (intensely); there was feeling *outside* of me that pervaded the room, the feeling of unworldly *wrong*. This feeling seemed not self-generated, but absorbed, as though I was being told to flee by voices of my ancestors, and they used my very blood as the receptor for the message. But before I could collect myself and take action, a strange thing happened: I saw that I was mistaken. I had somehow assembled the figure of the boy and the face from various objects: a bong, a sweatshirt, a pillowcase sliding between the bed and wall—part of the 'face' was defined by the leather strap and metal clamps of an adjustable roller skate! In the gloom, my mind had assembled a picture more quickly than my depth perception had adjusted. I chuckled with self-reproach. I looked away and blinked my eyes, and then looked back again, curious to see if I could reconstruct the scene now that I had 'unseen' it.

I needn't have worried. I saw the face again—I saw the face and it was a face, unquestionably, and it *pressed closer* to the foot of the bed. Its expression had changed as well: there was cruel challenge in the boy's eyes. The fear there had mouldered and spoiled, and defiance emerged from the dregs. His expression bespoke a horrid invitation to stay and 'see him away' again—and see what might come from that.

I did not. I gave in to my better judgment at last. I scrambled backwards and leapt to my feet on the landing. I glanced at the bed but saw no movement. I turned off the light and somehow retained the presence of mind to shut the door quietly, if no less firmly than I possibly could. There was, of course, no logic to hoping the closed door could protect me—yet hadn't I seen it move before? If there are rules, I do not know them. But I was damn sure the door would not open on its own.

I went back downstairs. Rollo was still in front of the couch. He watched me cross the room with no more than mild concern—though watching that same turn of his head only strengthened my first appraisal of the motion. With the same useless logic of protection I applied to the door, I hid under my blanket on the couch. I am surprised my flopping about didn't wake one of the others. Perhaps it did. I fell asleep quickly afterwards. That may seem unthinkable, but I was more drained now than ever. Another benefit of youth: being able to sleep no matter the circumstances given the right degree of exhaustion (a feat I cannot manage now). I even tried to stay awake. I watched the top of the stairs. I knew I was staring too long at the railing and that that was what caused me to see the straight line waver, as though something toyed at moving out from behind it. I knew that the flutter of my drooping eyelids made me see the shadows shift on the wall. I waited for Rollo to growl again but he did not. I remember thinking, *He was hiding in the pantry, and then he went to hide under his bed.* I don't know the source of the unnatural surety I had of either the original function of the Dungeon or of the boy's actions. I did not manage another coherent thought that night.

By the time I awoke in the morning Rollo had gone to his master's bed. When I went up to use the bathroom I saw that the bedroom door was once again open.

On our return trip several days later, we pushed through to Columbus without stopping; I did not return to that house.

Dark World

You may wonder that I did not relate the night's events to the others. I confess I did not see the point. Steve had lived in the house for a time already, and I thought that if he had not witnessed the phenomena himself by then, alarming him served no purpose. Whoever slept in that bed was clearly not 'sensitive'; it seemed best to leave the occupant 'in the dark'. I expect Hayes might have raised every alternative explanation that I have already detailed. Finally, my own doubts fostered silence. No matter how sure I was of everything that happened, part of me didn't *want* to believe, and I found myself reaffirming my excuses. If it weren't for that face, my conviction may have wavered. It did not; it does not. I have wondered since if ghosts are able to avail themselves of those optical illusions wherein they seem to appear. This may seem an odd argument—to hold up the alternative explanation in support of the phenomena— but if we speak of phantoms as beings of psychic energy peeking out from the hidden angles in the shadows, it makes sense to me that they might be spied most often through the *faults* in our perception. The sceptic will quibble that I wilfully ignored opposing evidence. You'll forgive me if I felt no sense of moral obligation that evening to persevere and attempt to 'unsee' that face. I do not feel my fear was ungrounded. I have never doubted that I was right to disengage when I did, and I have learned since that my conviction was correct.

At the time, the World Wide Web was in its infancy. None of my contemporaries had a home modem. Students wanting to use the internet went to a console at one of the university libraries. Only a few of my friends had begun to use email (I had not). The point being, I did not have the opportunity for casually browsing a gargantuan repository of useful and useless minutiae. There was no way to further research my encounter that did not include greater effort than I was willing to put forth. I have mentioned already that my lax attitude and devotion to other interests also allowed the matter to drift from my focus so that the mystery of that house faded quickly to the distance.

Recently, while sorting through some old boxes (and wondering how there were *always* more old boxes in my small house), I came across a cassette tape recorded by my friends (presumably in the Dungeon) and released on their cottage record label. I recognised immediately the address on North Congress scrawled on the paper tray card as being that of the house in which I spent one frightening evening. Having now both the address and the means to research the house at hand, I searched the internet for whatever answers it might provide.

At first I found nothing useful. Knowing the property value did me no good, and I soon discovered I lacked the savvy to identify prior owners; it seemed gaining that information would require the in-person rifling through of official records I had avoided twenty years ago, and though I am perhaps more responsible and motivated now, likewise am I busier and unlikely to find the extra time to follow that avenue. My search was not entirely without results, however. The house was mentioned in a forum on a website detailing various 'hauntings' in Ohio. I include the post from 'bobcatgrrl6' in its entirety:

One year when I was at OU I lived in a house at — N. Congress. Stuff used to turn on and off on its own and there was one room that never got warm. We used to joke we had a ghost but really we thought the wiring was bad. We were more afraid the house would burn down one night. We told the landlord but of course he didn't do anything. Then one time a hippie chick friend of mine was hanging at the house. All of a sudden she gets this crazy look. We ask her what's up and she says, 'Did you see that?' She gets up and creeps upstairs like she's following someone. We all laugh because we figure she's high, which wouldn't have been that unusual for her. A couple minutes later we hear her screaming her head off. We all run upstairs and she's halfway underneath my bed kicking like she's stuck. We drag her out and she's still screaming. We're all freaking out because we don't know what the hell is going on. My roommate even looks under the bed but there's nothing there. We have to hold on to her for like ten minutes to get her to calm down. She finally is just about able to start talking to us when she turns her arm around and we can all see these marks on her wrist—teeth marks. No doubt. Someone said, 'She bit herself!' but I didn't think so. The teeth marks looked like they came from little teeth. So she starts to freak again and we have to get her out of there. I took her home but she wouldn't talk about it.

The next day I go to see her to see if she's okay. At first I can't find her but her roommate swears she saw her go in her room and that she hadn't left. So I go back in to leave her a note. Then I hear something coming from the closet so I opened the door. She's scrunched down on the floor, hiding under some coats. She has a crazy look in her eyes. I talk real soothingly to her, but when I try to get her to come out she looks like she's mad and she's going to attack me. So I went out in the common room and waited. When she finally came out she seemed embarrassed but it was like she wasn't sure why.

She got weird and didn't talk much to anyone after that. Next year she dropped out or transferred. I don't know anyone who talked to her since then. I know whatever messed her up had something to do with what happened in that house. We all thought it was haunted after that. I moved out of that room and we left it empty. We kept the door closed but it would always open up again even though no one ever saw it happen. We never had any problems as crazy as that one time, but none of us wanted to renew the lease. I'd be curious to know if anyone else had any experiences there.

And so I think it's time to share. There may be someone more 'sensitive' than I who needs to know they are not alone.

I was unable to learn anything more as to the identity of the boy or the cause of the haunting—why he was frightened and against whom (and in what way) he might have rebelled. I think it likely just as well. My experience taught me not to go looking for monsters under the bed. If they choose to crouch there, leave them be—and hope they return the favour.

NOTHING BUT THE WAVES
Mark J. Saxton

WORK, for the majority of people, is a necessity rather than a pleasure. Many, if given the opportunity, would be happy to experience the life of the idle rich.

At least for a time.

When working, it's fair to say most are happier when they're busy. Active days tend to pass more quickly than quiet ones. Strange how we mortals so eagerly wish our lives away. Yet few of us enjoy being constantly rushed off our feet. There have to be limitations. Even machines need to be switched off now and again to cool and take a drop of oil. The odd slackening of business and a chance to enjoy a bit of a blow are usually welcomed. In the eyes of most people, it's inconceivable that an intelligent person of sound mind and professional qualification can possibly prefer to be quiet and idle at work, rather than active.

Nevertheless, there are those engaged in certain careers who consider a good day to be one in which they sit around on their backsides doing next to nothing. They would sooner see and speak to no one, despite their years of training and regardless of how much their inactivity makes the hours drag.

Hard to believe?

Just ask a doctor in a casualty ward, or any member of the emergency services. If their shift is one when the most exciting incident is a colleague spilling coffee on their lap, then that to them is a good day.

Being busy is a tragedy.

Nothing but the Waves

I've never worked in such a profession. I'm a man who always wants to be busy. Richard Reece, my old school pal and lifelong friend, was quite the opposite. He fell into one of the aforementioned categories.

Richard worked in a specialist role as a helicopter pilot back in the 1970s, a role for which he was destined.

When in school he was always the MAN. Cool, confident, brave. When we dared each other to climb a tree and jump to the ground, it was always Richard in the highest branches. When we played Chicken, he was always the last to move and with Knock and Run, he never flinched until he heard the footsteps in the hall. Perfect material for a pilot; tall, athletic, nerves of steel and a twinkle in his eyes that singled him out as having that certain something we can never put our fingers on, yet wish we had ourselves.

For a long period during his flying career Richard was with a unit known in the Royal Air Force under the abbreviation SAR, but commonly referred to as *Search and Rescue*. The SAR teams were not there for rescuing cats from trees. Their helicopters occasionally assisted fools in training shoes stranded on mountains, but more often stricken ships in troubled tides. In Richard's case that was most specifically in the choppy waters off the coast of Wales and out into the Irish Sea. For much of the time he was based at RAF Valley on the Isle of Anglesey. The base has received some attention in recent years due to the Duke of Cambridge and his pretty new wife being stationed there, but in Richard's day it was relatively unknown.

The units were originally set up during the Battle of Britain to assist downed air crews in the Channel. Spitfires and Hurricanes could be quickly replaced but experienced fighter pilots could not. By the 1970s, increased reliability and the lack of a Luftwaffe had rendered ditched aircraft something of an anachronism. The emergency call Richard's unit received on a dull autumn afternoon more than thirty-five years ago wasn't expected. It was unusual to be sent in search of a downed flight.

The crisis warning alerted them to the possibility of an aircraft having ditched in their vicinity. When the call was first received, Richard and his colleagues dreaded the thought it might be a large passenger jet with hundreds on board. It came as something of a relief when they discovered the aircraft responsible for reporting an engine malfunction before disappearing off the radar screens, was a Folland Gnat, a small training jet used by the military. It had just one person on board and had been en-route down the west coast of Scotland to their base on Anglesey.

One person or a hundred didn't matter to the team. Richard recalled with pride how swiftly and precisely they'd clambered into their Westland Sea King, ready to depart within minutes of receiving the call. Soon the deep thumping rotors became steady in the afternoon breeze. The grass and litter around the damp tarmac of the landing pad swirled and danced in the turbulence. Up they climbed, fat but steady, a huge yellow bumblebee in the grey November air. Quickly the ground fell away beneath them and within a few minutes the browns and reds of the autumn land rushed from below. All about the bulbous helicopter was the black jagged surface of the Irish Sea, a cold and unwelcome devourer of so many souls. It was crowned by a matching iron-coloured sky, appearing as hard and bitter as the mountains on the land vanishing behind them.

With Richard calmly at the controls they headed at some considerable knots in the direction last reported by the stricken aircraft. As they reached the vicinity and began to make low level sweeps there was nothing unusual to be seen. When he retired a few years ago, Richard told me the search and rescue teams of modern times have at their disposal so much techno-logical equipment, he would have given his right arm to have had half as much in his day. In comparison to his *old crate*, as he lovingly called her, modern helicopters would have been consid-ered science fiction in his early years on the job. For his devoted team on that autumn afternoon there were no night vision goggles, infra-red cameras or satellite navigation and tracking. They were just a group of fit men with their eyes staring out into the dim light. Men infused with a hope they would see something against the bleakness that might be a lifebelt or raft holding a survivor, in preference to a piece of wreckage or floating corpse.

As long as they could stay out above the dark waves, they did. Night came upon them too soon, the large fuel tanks nearly depleted. There was nothing to be done but return to RAF Valley and wait until daybreak. They'd seen no signs to suggest the craft had gone down in the sea where radar contact had been broken, but then a speeding jet could continue for miles below radar level before finally hitting the water. It was not unknown for a lost aircraft to pop up where it was supposed to be going, the pilot saying; 'Sorry about that chaps, had a little problem back there.'

It was however unlikely.

The team proposed widening the search area the following day. It was all they could do. They held on to the hope a cheery message would come through and order them to call off the search. The pilot might turn up safe and well; although the unlucky man would have to suffer the traditional embarrassment of dining in the officer's mess in his pyjamas, a punishment reserved for those forced to 'ditch their kite in the drink'.

By the time Richard's crew returned from their first sweep, a little more information had been received regarding the missing flight. A few of them there, Richard included, were rather shocked to discover the missing pilot was a man they knew. His name was Alfred Lande. As a test pilot he'd been involved in the development of the pioneering Hawker Harrier jump jet in the late 1960s, before moving on to become a pilot instructor. A respected and renowned member of the force, he was a large and jovial man with a square chin and a proper handlebar moustache straight from the pages of a Biggles comic. He also possessed the largest hands Richard had ever seen, large enough he recalled, to hold a couple of watermelons.

As an aside to relaying the story of Lande's infamous flight, Richard also told me an amusing anecdote about the older pilot.

It was at a training session in which he was involved some years before. He recalled him joking with some of the Royal Navy crews. The big man, hearty and forever pulling at the bushy handlebars beneath his nostrils, revealed the curious fact that despite serving for several years on the aircraft carriers *HMS Eagle* and later *HMS Ark Royal*, he couldn't swim so much as a yard. Like a brick, had been his actual words. When asked if that worried him; given he spent his life surrounded by water, he'd said not at all. Apparently, he knew he was destined to die on land and not in the cold embrace of any sea. His mother had been of a superstitious bent, with a penchant for tea leaves and crystal balls. After her only son joined the Royal Navy, she'd consulted a fortune teller. The old crone assured the mother her son would never die on any ship; she could read it on the cards.

And if the cards said such was so, that was good enough for his mother.

On the quiet, those who listened to his tale were quite astonished that for so intelligent a man, Lande also appeared to believe the gypsy nonsense. The story did the rounds, as such things do, earning him the nickname *Dry Lande*; although nobody Richard knew ever dared use it to his face. Those big hands would have many a flat-nosed heavyweight throwing in the towel.

With mixed sentiments, Richard admitted to me he'd found humour in the story too, but later felt sickened as he remembered those half-forgotten details. With Lande missing, he prayed the gypsy had been right, but the evidence suggested she was very, very wrong.

My old friend recalled an uneasy sleep that night, which was unusual for him. Even with the pressures of the world pressing down like a mountain, he always slept the sleep of angels. That night his rest was one plagued with a kaleidoscope of dreams. In fragments and snapshots, like a movie slipping in its projector, he was sitting with an audience of young pilots. All were very quiet, still and bolt upright on green plastic chairs with tubular legs. They watched Lande giving a lecture on a podium, his eyes fixed and unmoving whilst beneath the moustache his mouth spoke words Richard couldn't hear. The man's arms and great hands flayed wildly about, as if on nervous springs. All the while Richard was aware of freezing water lapping his ankles, deepening with every wave, but neither he nor the others about him could break their gaze from the man up front. Soon the water was up to his calves, his knees, his waist, as the entire room flooded. Salty water splashing at their chins, still they watched as the pilot instructor waved his hands, but still no sound could be heard, his dark staring eyes fixed and unmoving.

Richard only awoke, coughing and sweating, as the water entered his mouth.

The following morning the team resumed and widened their search. Needless to say the aircraft had not made it miraculously back and it was almost certain it had gone down in the unforgiving waters. There was little Richard could tell me about that second day of searching. Several sweeps of the area discovered nothing but the waves. Richard knew if the pilot was able to crash his bird on the surface with text-book perfection, it could remain intact and float for a time. The pilot would have a chance to escape, but there would be no debris spread over a large area for the search team to find.

At one point they did close in on some flotsam that from a distance looked to be a wing tip. Upon a low sweep it proved to be the lost board of a Welsh surfer, on its way to warmer climes.

Because of a certain camaraderie, they continued to search into the third day, although all knew it useless, even if Lande had bailed out or survived the impact. A big, strong, stubborn man, he wouldn't be a soul to give up easily. Even so, two and a half days in the November embrace of the Irish Sea stacked the odds against him.

But odds are not a perfect science.

Almost at the same moment the team was about to surrender to the inevitable, a gloved hand was thrust in front of Richard's face, pointing madly through the cockpit glass. Far off in a north by north-westerly direction, half a mile or so away, something bright orange was bobbing up and down on the jagged surface.

At once Richard changed direction and pointed the chopper on a straight path towards it. As they neared the object it became clearer. They could see the white circle of a face above the luminous collar of a life jacket.

Approaching and dropping in at low level, Richard saw two white dashes slowly moving backwards and forwards above the head of the person. With a feeling of exultation he realised they could only be the huge, plate-like hands of Lande as he waved to draw their attention. The handlebar moustache damply plastered across his upper lip was unmistakable. His face, although deathly pale against the darkness of the water, seemed to illuminate as they hovered in the air above him.

The waves were stirred by the downdraught of the rotors, the force aggravating an already angry sea. In the water instantly, the crew's diver reached the survivor whilst the winch man placed the cradle down on the spot in seconds. They lifted both on board in super quick time, a lot of back slapping and congratulating going on amongst the crew as they did so. Richard had a quick glance backwards and saw the large form of the downed pilot. He was very pale and weak, but so grateful in his eyes as the crew wrapped him up, eager to force some warmth into his icy body.

Jonathan, Richard's co-pilot and a colleague for some years, slapped Richard on the shoulder with delight as they turned the chopper around. As fast as the big crate would fly, it headed towards the Welsh coast. Jonathan radioed on ahead they were returning to base with a survivor and medical assistance was required urgently. Richard wanted to get his charge plumped up in fat hospital pillows, with a smiling, buxom nurse rubbing warmth into his limbs. Yet as hard as he pushed, the Sea King felt unusually ponderous as it snaked its steady way through the damp air. Richard tried to squeeze every last knot from the machine, but the helicopter felt drained and sluggish, the engine straining although the instruments registered no faults.

'How is he?' Richard asked Jonathan through the intercom as they came up to the land.

'Not good, but he's with us,' he answered.

Within moments they were above the base, the blue lights of an ambulance already pulsing through the cold drizzle of the day, dancing like fireflies on the speckled raindrops of the cockpit glass.

As he landed, cut the power and unclipped his safety harness, Richard looked over his shoulder into the large bay of the Sea

King. Instinctively he felt that something was wrong. Michael, the team's medic was making no effort to hide the concern on his face as he struggled with the pale and still form beside him. It was a look Richard recognised from old. The ambulance crew was also there, pulling themselves on board and within a few seconds the rear of the Sea King was full of busy people. Richard averted his gaze, silently looking at the sky through the rain-specked canopy of the craft. Nobody had to tell him. He knew they had lost.

For some, being busy is a tragedy. It has been mentioned. For Richard it had been a hectic few days. Such was and remains the nature of the job. Most of us are fortunately detached from such events. They exist only in the column inches of a newspaper.

It has to be put out of mind. Richard was no monster, but to dwell on failures was a cancer. The next time would be a success. If it were not, then he wouldn't dwell on that either. On he would go, every loss immediately forgotten, every success the fuel for the next. It was his job. Somebody had to do it.

A few days following the tragedy; his shift free to switch off as another carried their burden, Richard was sitting in the lounge of a local pub. It was a haunt the team often frequented when not on call. My old friend was having a few beers with his co-pilot Jonathan. Michael said he would be joining them later and sure enough he wandered in a little after nine o'clock. He quietly walked up to the bar. Instead of his usual Guinness, he bought himself a large scotch. Glass in hand, Michael walked listlessly to the table and sat heavily with a sigh. He was usually a cheerful man, I believe, with a round bright face and an endless store of jokes. To Richard it was obvious something was wrong and he asked him if he was alright.

Michael didn't have an ounce of rudeness in his body, but it was some time before he bothered to answer. He stared into his glass as if it housed all the horrors in the world. Eventually, without looking at his two friends, he said quietly; 'I've just come off the phone to Peter Kelly. Still hard to get my head around,' he whispered, sipping his scotch. 'Want to try and guess what he's just told me?'

'Not really, no,' Richard said. 'Why, go on. What's happened?'

Michael again was slow in answering. 'He was supposed to be performing an autopsy this afternoon, on that pilot you knew, the one we pulled out the drink the other day.'

'Alfred Lande?'

'Yeah, that's him.'

'What do you mean, was supposed to be?' Jonathan asked, slightly less patient than Richard.

Michael at first remained silent, his mood deep, a disturbed countenance barely hiding his thoughts. 'They went to the morgue where the body was stored,' he said. 'But when they opened the drawer in the refrigeration unit, it was empty.'

'What do you mean, empty?' Richard asked, unsure whether he'd missed something.

Michael took another sip of his scotch. 'It was bloody empty. The poor bugger's body has disappeared.'

'It's what?'

'It's gone. There was the smell of seawater; it *had* been there. But the tray was bone dry and your pilot friend conspicuous by his absence.'

There was silence for a second, a moment of dead air. Jonathan then made several comments that were rather rude, which I don't need to repeat. He finished off by asking; 'Who the hell would want to steal a dead body?'

'I never said it was stolen,' answered Michael. 'But it's not there now, that's all I know.'

'Well he certainly didn't stand up and leave, did he?' Richard butted in as Jonathan began to swear again. The conversation went on for some time, but nothing other than the obvious workings of a sick and twisted body snatcher could be blamed for the odd disappearance.

News of the poor man's missing body soon reached the local papers and then the wider national press. I myself vaguely recall it being on the BBC News many years ago. The Welsh police launched an investigation but to no avail. Despite many enquiries nothing was ever uncovered. The *Vanishing Pilot* as the press commonly referred to him, became just another news item to wrap up a fish supper. Wales's very own Burke and Hare remained elusive.

Over the next few months my friend Richard mused on the subject now and again, but was generally too busy to give it much consideration. It was only brought back to his attention a couple of years later when an unusual conversation took place one evening in the very same bar.

It was Michael's birthday and several of his friends were present, including Peter Kelly, the pathologist who was supposed to have performed the autopsy on Alfred Lande. Most people present were drinking and laughing. Peter, a fairly morose man who matched his patients, was having a conversation with a pretty but bored-looking nurse that Richard inadvertently overheard. He was telling the disinterested young lady the refrigerated compartment in the morgue, scene of the infamous body snatching, had in itself become something of an enigma to the staff in the hospital. Following the disappearance the compartment had been sterilised for re-use, but the smell of seawater remained, as if its aroma was infused within the metal. Worse still, as time progressed the stench became stronger and the whiff of salt water became tainted with a vile smell that could not be cleared despite frequent disinfections. Eventually, said Peter, the stench became so strong and putrid the compartment was sealed up. To that day it had never been used again.

Richard forgot about the conversation and in time, about the entire episode. It was only brought back to him when six years ago, a fishing trawler off the coast ran into difficulties not far from RAF Valley.

Richard by that time had retired, but he remained in close contact with the younger members of the old team who were still doing their bit. He heard of the incident a couple of days after it happened.

A helicopter had been called out to rescue the crew of a trawler. Happily the mission was a successful one. They pulled all the fishermen safely from the stricken vessel without any loss or injury. The stern had been damaged and the 'Lady Lucille' had taken on a great deal of unwelcome water when its nets had suddenly snagged on something large on the seabed, almost stopping the fishing vessel in her tracks with a great jerk. An operation was launched to investigate the potential hazard and a Navy diver discovered the object in question, still wrapped in the torn nets, was the wreckage of a crashed Folland Gnat that had been down there for a good few years.

The diver who found it had to report that unfortunately the pilot was still trapped in the jammed cockpit. Even after so many years in the cold dark waters, his moustache was still as grand as it had ever been.

Whether following their careful removal from the old wreckage, the remains were stored in a certain refrigeration unit in the morgue; or if indeed that container's seals have ever been broken, is something to which I don't have an answer.

It was a question Richard chose not to ask.

THE OLD BRICK HOUSE
Jayaprakash Satyamurthy

Sometimes, destiny is what you deserve, what you've always been a part of. Sometimes, it is just something you cross paths with by chance and can't shake off. That's the possibility that worries me the most.

The plaque on the boundary wall said 'Dunroamin' but I always thought of it as the dump. It was a tiny old Victorian cottage that was surely destined for demolition in the near future. It had once been a delightful two-storey red brick structure with a pretty garden; when I saw it, someone had painted the brickwork over in a sickly yellow that was faded and flaking. The roof had fallen in at various points, the windows were shuttered and the whole front garden smelled of stale urine and rotting vegetables. It was no better inside—dust and cobwebs had settled over everything, and I could see the turds and footprints of rats all over the floors. The heavy, wooden furniture seemed to have stood up fairly well over the years, but any upholstery was long gone, rotted or chewed away. On the other hand, there was still running water, the cottage had been electrified sometime in the 1970s and the wiring still worked, even if the lights were given to flickering. Once the cleaning lady was through with the place, it was just about bearable. Well no, not really. It had all the cosiness of a very small, dingy catacomb. But the four-poster bed was spacious and, once equipped with a new mattress, comfortable enough. The huge, lion-clawed brass tub in the bathroom was the only other feature of the cottage that met with my approval.

I didn't enjoy living there. I was used to bright, modern gadget-stuffed homes. I'd spent my childhood and teens in Hong Kong where my father worked as a manager in a mall. Even when I'd had to move back to the dreary old motherland for college I'd stayed in a flat in a plush new residential complex in Bangalore, which was then experiencing its first IT boom courtesy of the Y2K scare. I did an MBA in Australia afterwards, and then came back to Bangalore, where my father had arranged an internship for me at a friend's investment consultancy. My parents' flat had been let out and my father, planning for his retirement, insisted that he needed the lease money so I was forced to look for a place that I could afford on a fresher's salary. I stayed in a couple of single-room hellholes in working men's hostels for a few months before I begged my employer to help me find something a bit larger, which was how I wound up in the dump. He said it was an old family property that he hadn't got around to renovating or demolishing yet and that I would find it 'quaint'. That was when my heart started sinking. It well and truly plummeted to the depths of despair when I saw the place, but it was too late. I had been offered the dump free of rent as long as I paid the bills and it would be churlish to back out without at least giving it a shot.

So there I was, adrift in Dunroamin, spending my free time at the internet parlour up the street looking for another place to stay, another job, another life. My work was dull and sparse; I soon realised that investment consultancy was not my employer's primary occupation. I never did find out what his real business was, but the few accounts I was assigned were low in value and interest. I had a lot of time to stare idly into the middle distance, trying not to think too much about anything at all, least of all about the glowing arcades and malls of Hong Kong, the lavish bachelor parties of my college days, the wild nights in the hostel in Sydney, even less about my current circumstances, about the dump. After a while, this blankness became a familiar, comfortable state, one I could easily access whenever I wanted to.

That was why I thought she was a hallucination. I thought I had crawled too far back into my head and I was starting to crack up. Certainly, the first time I saw her, I didn't think of checking if she was real. It was just too far-fetched.

It was a Sunday morning and I had just finished bathing. I pulled on jeans and a t-shirt and stepped out into the first-floor corridor. I was standing there, feeling the blankness slide over my thoughts, when I saw a woman standing with her back to me. She was dressed in black jeans and a grey sweater-vest worn over a black shirt. Her hair was dark, glossy and tied in a high ponytail. She was standing a few feet away from me, her arms at her side, shoulders moving a little. She turned around, and I could see that she was crying. I stood aside as she walked past me and then turned to see where she was going. She had disappeared. I suddenly felt cold, but I ascribed it to the fact that I was still damp from my soaking in the old brass tub and must have been standing in a draught. I took a few tentative steps in the direction she'd taken. There was nothing there except a solid brick wall at the end of the corridor, so I gave up.

I saw her again a few times, always in that first-floor corridor, standing and crying, then turning around and walking away. Eventually, even in my numbed state of mind, I started to wonder what she was crying about, who she was walking away from and what she was walking towards. But mostly I just assumed it was a trick of my own mind and tried not to dwell too much on it.

The Old Brick House

Then, I got the letter. A firm in Dubai had accepted my long-shot job application. I was to join their marketing team in a month. I accepted and turned in my resignation at my father's friend's company. A week before I was to fly out of Bangalore, I called some of my college friends who were still in town and a couple of my colleagues over for a farewell party.

It was late at night and we'd downed several bottles of booze when one of my guests, Ajith, started telling a story. We'd all been fairly loud and raucous, but something in his voice quieted us down and compelled our attention.

ℰഠ

The Story in The Old Brick House

There was once a temple here, it doesn't matter to which god. It was rumoured that an ancient king had buried a treasure deep under the temple as an offering to the deity. Once a year, the idol was taken out of the sanctum and paraded through the streets by the junior priests before being brought back to the temple for a grand ceremony. Once, a group of desperate men decided to take advantage of this festival to find the buried treasure. There were three of them: Ranga, a veteran thief, past his prime but the brains of the operation, Gopi, slow in the head but tall and strong and Jehangir, the son of a deceased accomplice of Ranga's. They waited for the junior priests and devotees to leave on their procession before sneaking inside. Jehangir, who had never been inside a Hindu temple before, was taken by a sudden access of superstitious fear. God was one thing, but what if the creatures these infidels worshipped were actually djinns or efrits? He confessed his fears to Ranga, who grinned

143

from ear to ear. 'A dreamer, like your father. But he never let his dreams stand in the way of the task at hand. Honour his memory and be bold, son.' This little speech had the desired impact on Jehangir, who treasured his scoundrel father's memory and feared the respectable, dull shop assistant's life his mother had planned for him just a shade more than he feared the supernatural. 'Of course,' he replied. 'Did you ever doubt I would?' 'Then you won't mind being the first to enter?' asked Ranga. 'I was hoping you'd ask!'

So it was that Jehangir, only a yeoman thief, was the first to enter the temple that day. He crept in like a professional, making no sound and leaving no tracks. It was only inside, when a flicker of lamplight within the sanctum seemed to cast a menacing shadow on the walls, that he remembered his fears. Even then, he remained focussed on his task—to subdue and restrain the one man left in the temple, the aged high priest. He did this quickly and silently, although not as efficiently as one would have wished—but more of that later.

Once he had bound the old man, Jehangir whistled out to his comrades. Ranga and Gopi sneaked in, carrying their equipment. As the strongest, it was Gopi who would do the digging. Ranga had intuited that the treasure, if it existed, would be directly below the stone throne on which the idol usually sat. The three of them pushed aside the throne and smashed the tiles below it to reveal the earth beneath. Gopi set to digging. After what seemed an eternity to Jehangir, Gopi's spade hit something hard. He climbed out of the pit and Jehangir held a lamp directly over the pit as Ranga climbed in to investigate. He unearthed a large wooden chest. Jehangir threw down a rope. Ranga tied it around the chest and then climbed out. The three of them joined together in pulling it out, impelled by their excitement, even though Gopi's own sinews would have sufficed.

The Old Brick House

The trunk was locked. Ranga picked the lock and opened the lid. A glimpse of the glittering treasure within was enough to let him know their gamble had paid off. He slammed the trunk shut and then stuffed it into a gunny sack. Gopi heaved the loaded sack up onto his back and they were preparing to leave when it happened. The old man had managed to struggle out of his bindings—Jehangir's knots were not nearly as strong as they needed to be—and he surprised the thieves just as they were about to make their getaway. He would have raised an alarm if Gopi, thinking unusually quickly if not especially wisely, had not flung the sack, trunk and all, at him. It hit the old man with a dull thud and brought him down to the ground, his head pinioned under its weight. His limbs thrashed for a moment and then he was still. 'That's done it,' Ranga said. 'Don't just stand there staring, get that sack off him and let's take a look.' He gazed into the stricken priest's eyes, bulging out of the shattered, bloody head, felt for a pulse and put an ear to the old man's chest, but the verdict was obvious. 'Dead,' he said, unnecessarily. 'What do we do?' asked Jehangir. 'Why, bury him, of course,' replied Ranga, eyeing the hole Gopi had just dug. Gopi and Jehangir carried the body to the hole, dropped it inside and started filling the hole in while Ranga, determined to make their getaway swifter, divided the treasure into three sacks. The other two finished burying the priest and joined him. They slung their sacks over their shoulders and left the temple in different directions, having decided to meet at a rendezvous point outside town that night. They weren't sure how soon people would find that the priest was missing and it was best to avoid being seen in a group with a suspiciously large burden if the priest's absence was discovered before they had left town.

The streets were packed with devotees and it seemed as if the three would easily be able to mingle with the crowds and make good their escape. Only, they mingled too well. Time and again they found themselves drawn along with its momentum, their steps inexorably directed back towards the temple, the one place where they least wished to return. Gopi struggled the hardest, attempting to head down one detour after another, only to find the streets twisting and bringing him back to the procession. Ranga soon gave in to a sort of fatalism, ready to meet whatever fate had in store for him. Jehangir also gave up quickly, crying silently but keeping a tight grip on the hilt of a dagger concealed within his clothing.

They found themselves walking side by side, at the head of the procession. Ranga nodded at his accomplices, a devil-may-care grin dawning on his disreputable old face. Gopi nodded back, his face damp with sweat, eyes bloodshot. Jehangir tried to duplicate Ranga's grin, but it sat awry on his slim, young face. By now the crowd had stopped and the din of its chanting and drumming ceased as everyone stared at the three men who were entering the temple ahead of them. Cautiously, a few of the priests followed the trio, and then the rest of the crowd started to jostle their way in. Inside, the three men bowed down before a dark figure. The ceremonial flame had been lit and it leapt high and fierce, its restless light picking out details intermittently. The throne lay on its side, overturned and there was a great mound of earth where something had been dug up, or had dug itself out of the earth. The glow of the flame picked out the dark form in a sudden spotlight. It was the high priest, but his robe was covered in mud and his head was horribly malformed, pulped and bloody. Still, his eyes flickered in that livid light, keen and intent. He stood with his arms on his hips in a triumphant attitude as the three thieves started to crawl forward, still kneeling down. He began laughing when they dragged themselves into the flames one after the other, the assembled crowd staring in rapt horror, unable to speak or intervene. The old priest laughed for a long time; as long as it took for the screams of the dying men to subside. Then, he collapsed to the ground. Suddenly able to move again, the crowd rushed in.

The old man was dead.

Every man who had been there that day there would remember the priest's laughter and the cries of the burning men for the rest of his days.

ॐ

'What the heck?'

A clamour of voices rang out, asking Ajith where he had heard such a story, and why he had told it to us.

'What story?' he asked. At first we thought he was having us on, but it soon became clear that he was deadly earnest—he had no recollection of having told us the story and his voice had subsided to its usual nondescript timbre, no trace left of the resonant, mesmerising tone in which he had been speaking. We decided that we were all a lot more drunk than we'd realised and the party broke up soon afterwards.

I left for Dubai the following Saturday. My father retired and settled down in our Bangalore flat. I flew back and spent holidays with my parents a few times. When my father passed on, my mother went to live with my married brother in New York and we sold the flat. I put all thoughts of Bangalore, old brick houses, vengeful priests, disappearing women and the whole blank, pointless life I had lived far, far behind me. But Bangalore is not the sort of city you can completely shake off; it has a way of creeping back into contention. Nearly two decades after my time in Dunroamin, I was invited to participate in a seminar in Bangalore. My firm offered to pay all expenses, so I went.

I'd been told it was a fifteen minute drive from the airport to the hotel I'd been put up in. As my taxi drew nearer to my destination, it struck me that the area was familiar. I recognised a roundabout and a flyover. We passed a statue of some medieval king and it all fell into place. This was the same area where Dunroamin had stood! The taxi reached the hotel where I was to stay and I realised that this was the very street I used to live on. My father's friend must have sold Dunroamin at last, and someone had consolidated it with a number of other plots to build a lavish five-star hotel. There was a small shrine in a corner of the hotel compound—a noticeboard outside it informed me that the remains of a nineteenth-century temple had been found while the hotel was being built.

The conference was interesting enough, as these things go, and I made a lot of good contacts. On the penultimate day of my stay, I decided to have dinner in an open-air café in an extended terrace on the first floor of the hotel. It was reasonably early and there weren't many diners there yet. On a table a few feet away from me, a young Indian man in a light linen suit could be seen deep in conversation with an attractive blonde. I admired her until the waiter brought me my food. A while later, while I was wondering if my waistline could bear some dessert, I heard voices raised in anger. I looked up. The blonde woman's face was flushed and she was shouting at a person who was standing at her table, facing away from me. The man in the linen suit was nowhere to be seen. After a while, the person the blonde was shouting at turned around. She was a young woman dressed in black jeans and a grey sweater vest worn over a black shirt. Her dark, glossy hair was tied in a high ponytail. She was crying. I stared after her as she walked away from the café. I was sure I had seen her before, but the memory was vague and inconclusive.

The last day of the conference was a more relaxed affair—a few summing-up sessions, a closing ceremony and mixer. It was going to be a less taxing day and I was ready to unwind a bit. I should have been at a downtown nightclub with some of the crowd from the seminar, but I wanted time to myself, to recharge my batteries. If I hadn't been so determined to just relax, I would probably have thought things over a little more, until I had teased out the memory of the disappearing woman in Dunroamin. As it was, the waiter came back to my table and I decided to order a fruit salad and a gin and tonic. I was tossing back my second gin and tonic when I heard another outcry. Everyone was standing up, staring in horror. I looked up to see what had caught their attention. The young woman I'd seen earlier had climbed out onto the balcony of a room a few floors above the café, and set off to one side. As the voices around me rose in volume and desperation, she climbed out over the balcony railing and threw herself off. I ran to the edge of the terrace and looked down. I saw her lying on the paving stones below, spreadeagled like a tossed ragdoll, blood streaming from her head. I looked away, horrified, then looked back. Just for a moment, I thought I saw a ceremonial platform with a sacrificial flame at its centre. An old man in a filthy robe stood beside the flame, his head a bloody pulp in which the eyes could still be seen bulging from their sockets. A shadowy form emerged from the young woman's body and crawled towards the flames. The old man's shoulders heaved. He was laughing.

I managed to attend the last day of the conference, but I was dazed and listless. Everyone understood—I had witnessed a rather spectacular suicide, after all. Back in Dubai, I had a lot of leads to follow up and a promotion to chase. I tried to keep myself busy, too busy to think about what I had seen in Bangalore. But I knew I was a marked man.

I thought of all the people over the ages who'd been felled by fates they had never chosen. Why should I be any different? I'd seen something I wasn't meant to, and it had, in turn, seen me. Ajith's story was a challenge, a way of letting me know the game was on. Then, it had waited, watched, drawn me back in and let me go, just to show that it could. I was a loose end and I would be tied up, all in good time. I'd crossed paths with something and I couldn't shake it off. That was all there was to it.

THE PASCHAL CANDLESTICK
R.B. Russell

Wendy Owen received the phone call just before three in the afternoon, one weekday, not long before Christmas. The delivery driver claimed to have driven up and down Arkengarthdale without seeing any signs for Hackthwaite Lane, and he was now in Reeth. He was behind with his schedule, and was resolved to continue on to Richmond. He tried telling Wendy that she could pick up the package from a depot in Middlesborough at any time after ten the following day, but she pointed out that he was obliged to deliver before six that evening. She added that she had taken a whole day off work in the expectation of the delivery, and after a very long pause he reluctantly agreed to try again.

She gave the man detailed directions, telling him that he had to come back through Langthwaite, explaining that the turning for Hackthwaite Lane was immediately after the barn without a roof, and that the track up to Holme Cottage was adjacent to an old railway carriage used for storage by a local farmer. She made the man repeat it all back to her before he rang off; there was little chance of mobile phone coverage once he was out of Reeth.

It was almost completely dark when the van finally drew up outside the cottage. It was cold, and odd spits of rain were fleetingly visible in the beam of the vehicle's yellow headlights. The driver was angry about the state of the track, and frustrated that he would have to reverse back down it because there was nowhere to turn his vehicle. The 'package' was actually a large wooden crate, and, inevitably, the driver wasn't happy that he had to carry it around to the back porch, after they'd discovered that it was too wide to go in through the front door. But nothing, not even a bad-tempered driver, was going to stop Wendy from taking delivery of this; not after four years fighting for it through the courts.

She didn't feel able to open it up until the sound of the reversing van, and its headlights, had disappeared into the night. She felt rather exposed standing in the light of the open back porch, even though her nearest neighbours, the Johnsons, were several hundred yards away and in the other direction. The upper part of Arkengarthdale is sparsely populated, but on a clear night there are a surprising number of lights visible, pinpoints in the darkness, from various scattered cottages and farms. Not that this night was at all clear; the rain was getting heavier and the wind stronger.

Wendy felt momentarily helpless when it came to opening up the crate. But then she remembered the poker by the fire in the living room. She was pleased to find that it was exactly the right implement for levering the planks apart. The nails shrieked as they were pulled out of the wood, and the straw with which the crate was packed spilled out over the porch floor, and was soon whipped away by the rising wind, out into the black night. It was not long before she was able to remove the large, plastic-wrapped bundle that it contained.

She brushed down the object that she had pulled from the straw, before taking it inside and standing it in the middle of the kitchen floor. Then she went back out to clear up the porch. The remaining straw and all the loose planks went back into the crate which she dragged into the woodshed, where she planned to break it up for kindling. Returning to the house she went first to the living room where she drew the curtains and turned on the rather harsh overhead lights, before putting a match to the newly-laid fire. Only then did she bring through the plastic-wrapped object from where it had been standing in the kitchen. With the scissors from her sewing basket she cut away the protective plastic with great care.

Wendy made herself take the pieces of wrapping and put them in the wheelie-bin outside. When she came back in she locked both the front and back doors; she didn't quite know why. In the living room she put a couple of logs on the crackling fire, and only then did she dare to properly admire the sixteenth-century wooden paschal candlestick that she had inherited from her sister, Elizabeth.

It really was very beautiful. Five foot high and intricately carved, it stood on three feet that looked like those of a lion. The central column was almost classical, with swags of indeterminate fruit and flowers wrapped around it. It had not been restored; it showed the remains of the original polychrome paint, to which the firelight added its own suggestion of gilding. At the crown, the candlestick exploded into a riot of foliage with a wide flat top, upon which stood the remains of a very large, fractured candle which had obviously been damaged at some time during the four years it had been in storage.

Wendy moved the standard lamp away from her armchair and put the paschal candlestick in its place. It looked just as good as she had hoped it would. It was exactly as Elizabeth had once had it in her own, rather differently furnished living room. Wendy decided that finally everything was perfect, but then an icy shiver ran through her that she could not account for.

Holme Cottage is a traditional stone-built Yorkshire Dales house, and sits high on the south side of Arkengarthdale. That is, it faces north, and even in the summer it is rarely warm. With the rain thrown against the window that night, and the wind wuthering in the chimney, it was suddenly very cold in Wendy Owen's living room. Since she had added the logs, the fire seemed to be giving out no heat at all. In the cupboard she had a new candle ready for the candlestick (she had bought it some years ago from an ecclesiastical supplies company in London), but all that she could think of now was lighting what remained of the one already in place. She took the matches from the mantelpiece and with shaking hands coaxed the small black stump of a wick into reluctant life. It flickered and spat for several moments, but it did finally catch, and then the flame slowly pulled itself up and burnt with great certainty, despite the draughts.

The feeling of cold had been a momentary one. When Wendy turned off the ceiling lights, all at once the room seemed to be filled with an amiable golden glow out of all proportion to the size of the flame. She sat in the armchair with the fire warming her on one side, and on the other the candlestick throwing its soft illumination on her book. The wind had changed direction; it was no longer making strange noises in the chimney, but was whistling around the front door out in the hall. The rain at the windows was quite insistent, but a calmness and contentment came over Wendy as she read by the light of the paschal candlestick.

స

Elizabeth Owen had been the senior buyer for a large department store in Darlington, and her 1970s-built house in Yarm had been furnished in an ultra-contemporary style, with a couple of twentieth-century design classics of which she was very proud. Wendy could appreciate her sister's good taste, but was always glad that Elizabeth never made any comments about the ad-hoc way in which Wendy had put together the furnishings in Holme Cottage. The one item upon which the two sisters were in sympathy was the only true antique that Elizabeth owned; the candlestick that always stood so elegantly beside the armchair in her spacious living room. She had recklessly paid a great deal of money for it when she had been much younger, and she said that there was a story attached to it. One day, she always teased Wendy, she would tell her the tale, but she never did. All Wendy knew was what her sister had once said in an unguarded moment; that it was a souvenir of a perfect few weeks abroad, with friends, before she had been married.

Wendy nodded-off over her book, and when she woke up she was surprised to discover that it was after midnight. She decided not to blow out the candle until the last minute, and instead went out to wind up the clock in the hall, and to make herself a hot drink to take up to bed.

As she stood waiting for the kettle to boil, the unfortunate memory of Elizabeth's husband, Trevor, forced itself upon her. Elizabeth and Trevor's marriage had never been a happy one, but both were too stubborn to call it a day until just before Elizabeth's death of a heart attack, aged only forty-five. Wendy had known Trevor when he had been studying law at university, and, unfortunately, she had effected the introduction between them. Wendy never could stand the man; she would only visit Elizabeth when she was sure that he was up in Newcastle, where he worked as a solicitor. When they did occasionally meet, Trevor made his own loathing of Wendy quite obvious.

To Wendy's annoyance, Elizabeth had been very generous in her Will to Trevor. She had made a few specific bequests: her set of Marcel Breuer chairs to a friend, some Picasso prints to their brother, Tom, and her jewellery to Tom's wife. The candlestick was for Wendy, of course, because she had always so admired it. . . . It was all very straightforward until Trevor decided to contest the Will. In spite of inheriting most of Elizabeth's assets, he also wanted the candlestick!

Wendy had been forced to meet him with her solicitor, and Trevor produced a receipt for the candlestick, dated ten years previously. Wendy protested that Elizabeth had acquired it before she'd even met Trevor, and so it went to court. Even when Tom discovered a photograph taken in Elizabeth's front room, showing them all there one Christmas, with the candlestick in the foreground, Trevor refused to back down. Burnt into the lower left hand corner of the photograph in orange numerals was the date that exposed Trevor's lie.

Wendy took her hot drink upstairs, turning the lights off after her, still annoyed that the legal case with Trevor had cost her more in solicitors' fees than the candlestick was probably worth. But she had not been going to give up the fight on principle! She asked Trevor, at one point, when they were alone, what he intended to do with the candlestick if he managed to obtain it. Unbelievably, he had said that he wanted to chop it into firewood and burn it! It made Wendy shudder to remember the hatred the man had displayed. She had always thought him ugly, but the barely concealed rage in his weasel-like face made him look positively evil. Even now she could not decide whether the vengeance was meant to have been at Elizabeth's expense, or hers.

Although on the edge of sleep, with the bedside light switched off, Wendy could not stop thinking about how full of anger Trevor had been. When he was killed in a car accident over a year ago Wendy hoped that his claim on the candlestick would drop, but it had still dragged on for another twelve months until his estate had been settled.

The Paschal Candlestick

Wendy slept surprisingly well considering how agitated her thoughts had been before falling asleep. When she came downstairs the following morning the flame was still determinedly burning in the wreck of the old candle. In the living room there was a surprising amount of residual warmth. Always a little worried about fire, Wendy was appalled that she had forgotten to blow the candle out before going to bed, and did so now with alacrity. The room seemed suddenly colder, but she threw back the curtains and went about her morning routine before leaving for work.

All day Wendy was in something of a dream, thinking about Elizabeth and Trevor, alternating between sorrow and loss, and an anger that she knew to be a waste of emotion. When she returned that evening, Wendy carried the candlestick out into the kitchen so that she could remove the old, broken candle. The new candle she had bought was very substantial, and of just the right proportions, but first she had to hollow out a hole in the bottom so that it would fit over the large metal spike on the top of the stick.

The weather had improved steadily during the day and the wind had died down. Now there were no draughts in the house the flame was even taller than before as it illuminated the living room. Wendy made herself supper and ate it in the armchair, listening to the radio. Later that evening she dug out her family photo album. Leafing through it, with Elizabeth's candlestick at her side, she felt nostalgic for a past that seemed more distant than ever. Looking at the familiar images of her grandparents made Wendy smile, although the sentiment she felt when looking at the photographs of parents, brother and sister, was mainly sadness.

Wendy turned to the last leaf of the album and saw the studio photograph of Elizabeth that had been taken on her thirtieth birthday. Wendy had always admired it, but it was almost as though she had never before looked at it properly; Elizabeth was so beautiful, and so full of vitality and humour. Wendy remembered the silk dress Elizabeth was wearing, and wondered what had happened to it. Thrown away, she expected. But the pendant, with the tiny opals, would belong to Tom's wife now. Would it be appreciated? Probably; Wendy liked Tom's wife.

And then Wendy suddenly discovered that she was crying: it was so painfully wrong that her beloved sister was no longer alive.

She wiped away the tears that blurred her vision. She closed up the album and sniffed, resolving to do something practical that would stop her from dwelling on the past. She put the album on the floor while she banked-up the fire. Then she went out into the kitchen where she started on the process of making a Christmas cake. 'Buck up, old girl!' she said out loud, and then realised that talking to herself was not a good sign.

A half hour later the cake was in the oven, and Wendy went back into the living room to check on the fire, which was low. The candle was burning strongly, though, and in its kindly light she saw the photograph album where she had left it on the floor. Caught between the idea of adding more wood to the fire and picking up the album, while at the same time thinking about her sister, Wendy bent down and seemed to see sitting in the armchair, out of the corner of her eye, Elizabeth.

Wendy's heart stopped and she could not breathe. She clutched her chest and had to put her hand out to the mantelpiece to steady herself. Her eyes had only shifted momentarily from the armchair, and now it was empty.

A second later and her heart seemed to miraculously re-start itself. She was able to gracefully draw in a breath.

The Paschal Candlestick

Wendy Owen was a woman of good sense. She sat down on the small settee normally reserved for visitors and recovered herself, trying to calm her heart-rate. Not for one moment did she take her eyes off the armchair. In her mind she rehearsed how she might explain what she had seen to somebody like Tom. Words like 'ghost', 'vision', even 'hallucination' wouldn't impress a rationalist like him. She told herself that in the brief instant she had seemed to see Elizabeth, her sister had been sitting there just as in the studio photograph. She could imagine Tom patiently explaining to her that, in trying to do several things at once, she had simply confused reality with imagination. Wendy could hear Tom telling her that, if she had seen anything at all, she must have projected on to it the thought of the photograph in her mind.

Wendy was already feeling much calmer. She had been startled, but she didn't think that she had really been frightened. In fact, the apparent glimpse of Elizabeth seemed to bring her some comfort; as though, somehow, Elizabeth was with her, in the room. Wendy certainly wouldn't tell Tom that! She knew she was being silly; it was obvious that her grief for her sister was still strong, even after all these years.

In the kitchen the oven alarm was ringing to let her know that the cake was ready. Had more than an hour already passed? She made herself go and take out the cake, and she left it on the side in the kitchen to cool. She found a dozen little household chores to do before getting herself ready for bed. That night, though, she did not forget to blow out the candle. The flame was burning resolutely; all was absolutely still outside and there were no draughts in the house. She blew out the candle only at the last possible moment, and hurried up to bed.

∞

Dark World

When Wendy awoke she instinctively knew that something was wrong. It was absolutely dark and perfectly quiet. The faintly luminescent hands of her bedside clock suggested that it was past three in the morning. Something had woken her, but she didn't know what it could have been.

Then she heard the slight noise from downstairs and was immediately terrified. It was the sound of metal, like the poker in the grate. She had an intruder, in the living room.

Wendy was terrified. Her heart was racing, but alongside fear was a hard-headed determination to escape. She slipped out of bed on the side of the room where the floorboards did not creak, and carefully made her way to the door. There was no light in the landing. If she heard anybody on the stairs, she decided, there was always the bedroom window for escape, although the bushes below wouldn't receive her very comfortably.

At any moment she expected the beam of a burglar's torch to probe the stairway. But then there was another sound, like a heavy item of furniture being moved. There was no doubt that the intruder was still in the living room. Wendy found it difficult to keep her composure, but she was able to tiptoe quietly to the head of the stairs, and then slowly descend. The front door was her goal; she knew the lock so well that she could open it and be outside in an instant. She just had to get to the door before he did. . . . And then, once outside, she would have to jump the garden wall and run across a field before she reached her neighbours, the Johnsons. Wendy congratulated herself on being so clear-headed when she was so scared. She was confident she could make it in the dark, even barefoot, without being caught by anybody.

The Paschal Candlestick

The last tread at the bottom of the stairs creaked as she put her weight on it. Wendy stopped, stifling her rising panic. But the sound she had made was probably not audible to whoever was in the living room; they were now muttering loudly to themselves.

A moment later and Wendy was at the front door. In two very quick, confident movements it was unlocked and opened, but the rush of cold air that prickled all over her skin came from within the cottage, not without. She turned, and in the dark of the hallway she could see the figure looming over her with the massive paschal candlestick raised up, ready to be brought down upon her head. . . .

∞

Wendy did not feel able to explain to the Johnsons exactly what she thought she had seen. She fled the house, and her neighbours seemed to take forever to respond to the hammering on their door. They called the police, who turned up half an hour later. Once they had investigated, they reported that the front door of Holme Cottage was wide open and that there was a big old candlestick in the middle of the hall floor, but otherwise nothing seemed to be amiss.

Wendy returned to her house the next day with Mrs Johnson, once it was fully daylight. They drank several cups of tea until Wendy said that she would be fine left on her own. She knew that she had a few hours to decide what to do, before it became dark. Initially she was certain that she had to take the candlestick outside and chop it up for firewood, but that would have been what Trevor wanted.

Wendy set the candlestick back in its place by the armchair and lit it. There was little noticeable illumination of the living room at first, but as night fell it was steadily filled with a warm, honey-coloured light. Wendy walked around the room, came in and went out, never looking directly at the armchair, always hoping for some sideways glimpse of her sister. She didn't see anything, but eventually she realised that the light of the candle was reassurance enough; it seemed to offer the comfort, even the protection, she hoped for. But it would have to be kept constantly lit, despite the fire risk, and she would have to guard against it ever going out once it was dark inside the house. For it had been in the night, with the candle extinguished, that she had seen the stick raised up, in the hands of the pale, pinched, hate-filled figure that had been so hideously suggestive of Elizabeth's ex-husband, Trevor.

NINTH ROTATION
Stephen Holman

Earl Grey crossed the threshold of the Medici Arts Academy at 8am on a Tuesday morning, with a familiar tightness in his chest and mild nausea in his stomach. He knew, from three months, experience, that the sensations would be only partially relieved by the mug of hot coffee that was, at that moment, first and foremost in his mind.

Earl traversed the main teaching area, heading towards the stairs leading up to the instructors' mezzanine. The journey meant weaving his way through a slow-moving herd of glassy-eyed teenagers who were also arriving to start their day. Despite its imposing name, the Medici Arts Academy was no seat of higher learning, but an inner city, public charter high school, catering to kids from sixth grade through twelfth. Though public, and therefore under the jurisdiction of the Los Angeles School Board, the fact that Medici had its own charter meant that it could offer alternatives to LA's standard education program. Earl's presence at the school was part of that alternative. He wasn't an instructor; he was an artist, hired by the school to enhance the kids' awareness of art, both in historical terms and (supposedly) to inspire through his own example.

Earl ascended the stairs to the mezzanine and walked towards the small kitchenette where instructors habitually clustered to escape during the five minute morning break and half hour lunch. The escape was only partial; there were no classroom walls in the Medici Arts Academy. The building had once been a clothing factory and the conversion from sweatshop to public school had been achieved with minimum expenditure. Despite— or perhaps because of—the daily presence of three hundred kids in the building, the spirits of whirring sewing machines were still able to make their subtle presence felt.

The mezzanine was empty. None of the other teachers had yet arrived. Earl made a beeline for the industrial sized coffee machine, and switched on the heater, intending to brew a fresh pot. Raising the large coffee urn, he realised that it was still half full of cold coffee brewed the day before. Abandoning his initial plan, he filled a mug with the rank fluid, stuck it in the microwave, hit the one minute button, and headed towards his teaching area to unpack his bag.

Leaving the kitchenette meant momentarily venturing back into the teenage jungle for a space of twenty paces, and the moment he did so, Earl regretted it. A tubby young boy with frizzy, carrot red hair suddenly entered his peripheral vision and stopped in front of him, blocking his path.

'Can you see this picture I drew?'

His mind fixed solely on his microwaving coffee, Earl waited impatiently as the boy reached into his bag and pulled out a creased sheet of paper. He held it flat for Earl to see. It was a primitive, graceless, pencil sketch of two battling figures, both of whom were wielding swords. No, scratch that. Light sabres. The rough, geometric outline of the larger figure's head had triggered the revelation that this was an intended portrayal of Darth Vader. Ergo, the scrappy character next to him must be Luke Skywalker. Conclusion: light sabres, not swords. The drawing contained no foreground elements. No background details. No sense of perspective. And extraordinarily little talent or imagination.

'Nice,' said Earl. 'Keep up the good work.'

Earl pushed past the boy, walked into the semicircle of chairs that defined his designated teaching area, and put down his bag with a sigh. It was now 8.05 am and already he felt tired. Teaching art history to high school children was not a profession for which Earl felt himself suited. Some were born to teach; others were born to create, and Earl had, from an early age, felt a deep conviction that he was born for the latter. Admittedly, having parents who were both successful artists might well have influenced this conviction, and yet Earl himself had experienced some degree of success in the fine art world. This success had peaked in his late thirties, however. The year 2000 had ushered in an era of minor disappointments that had accumulatively eaten away at his confidence. So, now here he was, somehow approaching fifty, and confusingly trapped in a career cul-de-sac that exhausted him so utterly that all recent attempts to initate artistic endeavours after work, or even at weekends, had sputtered into inertia. So much for inspiring through his own example.

Why he'd ever applied for this job to begin with was actually something of a mystery to Earl. Was it a misguided urge to 'give something back' to society? Or simply financial panic? He still wasn't sure. Why the school had accepted him was an even greater mystery; Earl had no previous teaching experience and certainly no teacher credits—usually essential in landing a job in the LAUSD school system. He got the impression, however, that the school principal, Alastair Gillespie, a rebel by nature, and a trail-blazer in the field of progressive education, had rather enjoyed the challenge of finding a way around the LA school board ruling. He'd done it by renaming Earl's job position. Earl Grey wasn't actually an 'art history teacher' or even an 'artist-in-residence' at the Medici Arts Academy; the official description of the work he did here was 'humanities enhancement'. Earl hated the title; he felt it belittled him. It gave fuel to a nagging suspicion that taking this job had been the biggest mistake of his life.

The distant ping of the microwave alerted Earl to the fact that his coffee was now hot and ready to drink. He headed quickly back to the kitchenette, which was now slowly filling with miscellaneous instructors, nodding silently to one another as they doffed hats and jackets, and prepared themselves for the coming onslaught.

8.30 am. First Rotation. It was another of Alastair Gillespie's naming quirks that nothing at the Medici Arts Academy should be known by its common appellation. Thus, teachers were 'instructors', pupils were 'scholars' and classes were 'rotations'. All a little pretentious, Earl thought, but hey, not half as bad as Starbucks naming its smallest coffee size, 'tall'.

First Rotation lasted forty-five minutes. This was followed by Second Rotation. Then the five minute morning break. Then two more forty-five minute rotations. Then lunch. Then four more rotations, with only a five minute 'meditation period' between the first two and second two. Earl taught the same exact lesson in each rotation—but to a different set of thirty kids—all of varying grades and ages. Noise level had to be kept as low as possible due to the lack of classroom walls, and much of Earl's teaching time was spent shushing and promising potential punishments to kids who dared talk during class.

Kids, Earl had been told by the other instructors, had an obsessive compulsion to communicate with each other and would go to any length to do so. They weren't adults, not even college students; they were kids, and kids find it difficult to control themselves. Earl tried not to take interruptions to his art history monologues personally, but still found the constant outbreaks of whispering and giggling, stressful and offensive. By the time he left the building after an eight hour day, having taught the same art lecture eight times, back-to-back, to eight different combinations of thirty unruly kids, he was always dizzy with exhaustion.

'In contrast to the Neoclassical perfectionism of his chief rival Ingres, Delacroix took his inspiration from the art of Rubens and painters of the Venetian Renaissance, with an emphasis on colour and movement rather than clarity of outline and modelled form. Dramatic and romantic content characterised the central themes of his later life, and led him not to the Classical models of Greek and Roman art, but to travels in North Africa, in search for the exotic. As well as being friend and spiritual heir to Theodore Gericault, Delacroix was inspired by Lord Byron, with whom he shared a strong identification with the "forces of the sublime"—of nature in violent action.'

Brrronggg! Brrronggg! Brrronggg! Earl's class was brought to an abrupt end by the sound of the school bell. End of First Rotation. The teenagers seated in front of him immediately leapt to their feet.

'Sit!' commanded Earl. The teens reluctantly sat.

'You may go,' Earl growled. The kids stood again and began to shuffle off to their next class. Earl turned and began to scan back through the jpeg images of Delacroix's paintings on his computer, readying himself for the imminent start of Second Rotation. His concentration was interrupted by a youthful voice close behind him.

'Can you see this picture I drew?'

Earl glanced over his shoulder. Standing next to him was the curly-haired kid who'd accosted him earlier. The boy was holding out the same drawing he'd shown Earl less than an hour ago.

'Didn't we already have this conversation?' Earl said, rummaging through the jumbled list in his head, trying to put a name to the boy's face. Remembering the names of three hundred teenagers in the three months he'd been at the school had not been an easy task. Some of the less prominent personalities had still not imprinted themselves successfully, and this young lad was apparently one of them.

'Go to your next rotation,' Earl told him. 'You'll be late.'

As he turned back to his computer, Earl caught a quick glimpse of the drawing. It did seem to have changed a little. Luke Skywalker had grown shorter and a little plumper, and the geometric shape of Darth Vader's helmet was now less distinct. His cloak had also been erased. The boy must have been working on it during math class.

Second Rotation.

' "Give me a Prussian Blue and I could make mud from the sewers of Paris look like a virgin's pale flesh." '

Earl looked around at the semi-circle of youthful faces. Somebody giggled.

Virgin. Hee hee. Earl kept at it.

'What do you think Delacroix meant when he said that?'

Silence.

'What do you think he was talking about? Hmm?'

Silence.

'Does anyone know what Prussian Blue is?'

Silence.

'Has anyone ever heard of Paris?'

Two hands sluggishly raised.

'Hallelujah. Well let's begin there and start filling in some gaps, shall we?'

Ninth Rotation

Five minute break. Then Third Rotation. Same again. Delacroix. Prussian Blue. Forces of the Sublime. Mud from the Sewers of Paris.

Fourth Rotation. Delacroix. Blue. Mud. Sublime.

Brrronggg! Brrronggg! Brrronggg! Lunch break. Thank God. Earl dismissed his 'scholars', quickly turned off his computer, fumbled in his bag for the plastic tub containing his sandwich and headed towards the instructor area. Suddenly the boy was in front of him, blocking his way. Thrusting forward his sheet of paper.

'Can you see this picture I drew?'

Earl looked down at the small, plump figure, trying to size him up. Was he being serious or was this another ploy to annoy the uptight art history instructor? The boy didn't look as if he had the gumption to attempt such a dare on his own. Had other boys put him up to it? Earl glanced around. No one else was paying any attention. He looked down again. The boy's face was blank, inscrutable. Marco? Marshall? Earl still couldn't remember his name.

'Okay. What are you up to? What's going on here?'

The boy continued to hold out the paper. Earl found his slightly vacant stare unsettling. He glanced down at the sketch. Again it seemed to have changed. Darth Vader had shrunk a little and his clothes looked more contemporary. Luke now had curly hair and had lost his light sabre.

'I do not critique scholars' personal artwork, and you shouldn't be doodling during school hours. If I see this drawing again, I will have to confiscate it. Now put it away and go to lunch.'

Earl pushed past the boy. He felt tense. Needing to unwind, he ignored the other instructors in the lunch area and sat down at a table on his own. He opened his lunch box and gazed out through the mezzanine railings at the sea of human hubbub on the floor below. The sight disturbed him. Averting his eyes, he tried to relax by focussing his thoughts solely on his ham sandwich.

Fifth Rotation. Delacroix. Delacroix. Forces of the Sublime. Mud from the Sewers of Paris. Did the life of this dead painter mean anything to these twenty-first-century teenagers? Did painting itself matter any more at all in this era of jpegs, instagrams, soundbites and ringtones? Picasso, in the first twenty-five years of his life, had witnessed the invention of steam turbine engines, cars, planes, movies, light bulbs, x-rays, machine guns and the theory of relativity. He had painted 'The Demoiselles D'Avignon' in response. The result had been to propel the respectable art of academic figure-painting into the industrial age. To have cynical smart-asses drag it, kicking and screaming, through fifty dynamic years of radical deconstruction and finally leave it burned out and washed up in the dead zone of postmodernism. Art was finished. Now these kids had nothing but consumerism to inspire them. That and the reheated remnants of artistic triumphs from ages past, dished out to them by guys like Earl, themselves disillusioned and washed up. They were all dead, or might as well be.

Announcement over the speaker system:
'Sixth and Seventh Rotations will be combined this afternoon. Scholars go to Sixth Rotation and remain in your seats when the Seventh Rotation bell sounds.'
What? What did that mean? Earl looked over at the science class that was being taught on the other side of the Mezzanine. The science teacher caught his eye, grinned and shrugged. Don't

ask me, the shrug seemed to say. Nobody knows why anything happens around here.

Earl groaned. Combining Sixth and Seventh Rotations meant, presumably, that he would have extra kids in his next class, and also mean that he would somehow have to extend his Delacroix lecture from forty-five minutes to an hour and a half. This sort of schedule-juggling happened a lot at Medici. Most instructors seemed unfazed by it, but Earl, still somewhat new to teaching and reliant on the structure of his carefully-planned classes, found it extremely stressful.

Combining Sixth and Seventh Rotations also meant that he would be dealing with Hugo and Emporio Burton for an hour and half; two brothers from a family of twelve kids, all of whom were named after perfumes or colognes. Emporio, the eldest, had told Earl on his second day at the school, that he and his brothers' plan for when they had left school was to start a gang and take over LA. Earl had laughed at the joke, but since then, had become less and less sure that it was one. Hugo and Emporio, both clearly opposed to art appreciation of any kind, had apparently seen Earl's art history class as a testing ground for their takeover plans. Using a mixture of pupil intimidation and instructor demoralisation, they had disrupted every art history rotation they'd attended since September. Their various ploys included kicking other kids when Earl wasn't looking, asking totally unrelated questions and addressing Earl as Mister Teabag. The next ninety minutes would be gruelling.

And what was worse . . . the boy was back. When the kids had arranged themselves on the seats, Earl looked around and saw him. Seated cross-legged on the floor, silently staring, still holding his drawing. Ignoring him, Earl started his lecture.

Twenty minutes into the rotation, Earl looked up. Emporio's hair was on fire. Flames crackling. Earl stared at the boy, entranced. An ex-girlfriend had once accidentally set her hair on fire at a dinner party by bending too low over a candle flame. For a second the shocking memory overwhelmed him. The girl shrieking. The expressions of panic. Earl blinked. The flames were gone.

'Be QUIET!' he shouted. Emporio looked astonished.

'I wasn't talking.'

The other kids smirked. Earl tried to regain his composure.

' "Give me a Prussian Blue and I could make mud from the sewers of Paris look like a virgin's pale flesh." '

The boy held up his sheet of paper.

'Can you see this picture I drew?'

'Get out! You're not supposed to be in this rotation!'

Earl turned to his computer and pretended to search for something on the menu. When he turned back around the boy was gone. Thank God. Earl picked up his notes and noticed that both his hands were trembling.

Brrronggg! Brrronggg! Brrronggg! Eighth Rotation had come and gone. Earl had somehow made it through his final forty-five minutes, feeling the whole time as if he was talking in his sleep. Blue. Sewers. Sublime. Brrronggg! Brrronggg! Brrronggg! The end of the day. With a sigh of relief, Earl dismissed the kids and slowly began to pack up his things. Suddenly the speaker system crackled. The voice announced:

'All scholars proceed to Ninth Rotation.'

NINTH Rotation! What? There *was* no Ninth Rotation! What was this? Another change that no one had told him about? Damn this place! This was the last straw. Tomorrow he would hand in his resignation and apply for a job at Starbucks. Earl turned shakily, ready to receive his ninth round of reprobates. As he did so, he realised that the school had become uncommonly silent. Only one boy sat on the semi-circle of seats in front of him.

'Is this it?' asked Earl. 'Just you?'

The boy thrust forward his picture. Earl took it and stared at it. The two figures had now fully transformed; no longer scrappy Star Wars characters but realistic depictions of himself and the boy. Rather well drawn, he observed. Earl felt dizzy. His chest hurt. The picture rose up towards him. A burst of white light erupted inside his head.

And suddenly it was the night before. He was inside the picture, inside his car, in the school parking lot. He was leaving work an hour later than usual, thanks to an impromptu meeting he'd been asked to attend. It was dark. Groups of kids, the ones who stayed for after-school programs, were still lolling about. He felt exhausted. Frustrated. Angry. He needed to get out of here. Now. He honked his horn. Move out of the way! Earl backed out of his parking spot and lurched towards the gate. In his rear view mirror, he noticed one of the older girls give him the finger. Couldn't be sure who it was in the dark. Damn it. He pressed down on his accelerator the second he was out of the gate and, turning right, shot down the road towards a residential area—a route he favoured over using major streets during rush hour. At the second junction, the street light was out. There was road construction work going on. A large ditch. A hastily constructed barricade. Momentarily confused, Earl had taken the corner a touch too early and run his car up onto the sidewalk. He'd felt a slight impact, heard a thunk somewhere on the rear passenger side, and assumed he'd bumped against a traffic cone. Should he stop and check? Just in case? No. Purging the thought from his mind, he'd swerved back onto the road and carried on driving.

Earl slowly opened his eyes. It was hard to see anything any more. He tried to speak, but found he couldn't. The boy stood over him. Smiling down at him. Forgiving him.

Martin. That was his name.

WHEATFIELD WITH CROWS
Steve Rasnic Tem

Sometimes when he sketched out what he remembered of that place, new revelations appeared in the shading, or displayed between the layering of a series of lines, or implied in a shape suggested in some darker spot in the drawing. The back of her head, or some bit of her face, dead or merely sleeping he could never quite tell. He was no Van Gogh, but Dan's art still told him things about how he felt and what he saw, and he'd always sensed that if he could just find her eyes among those lines or perhaps even in an accidental smear, he might better understand what happened to her.

In this eastern part of the state the air was still, clear and empty. An overabundance of sky spilled out in all directions with nothing to stop it, the wheat fields stirring impatiently below. Driving up from Denver, seeing these fields again, Dan thought the wheat nothing special. He made himself think of bread, and the golden energy that fed thousands of years of human evolution, but the actual presence of the grain was drab, if overwhelming. When he'd been here as a child, he'd thought these merely fields of weeds, but so tall—they had been pretty much all he could see, wild and uncontrolled. But when he was a child everything was like that—so limitless, so hard to understand.

In the decade and a half since his sister's disappearance, Dan had been back to this tiny no-place by the highway only once, when at fifteen he'd stolen a car to get here. He'd never done anything like that before, and he wasn't sure the trip had accomplished much. He'd just felt the need to be here, to try to understand why he no longer had a sister. And although the wheat had moved, and shuddered, and acted as if it might lift off the ground to reveal its secrets, it did not, and Dan had returned home.

Certainly this trip—driving the hour from Denver (legally this time), with his mother in the passenger seat staring catatonically out the window—was unlikely to change anything in their lives. She'd barely said two words since he picked her up at her apartment. He had to give her some credit, though—she had a job now, and no terrible boyfriends in her life as far as he knew. But it was hard to be generous.

Roggen, Colorado, near Interstate 76 and Colorado Road 73, lay at the heart of the state's grain crop. 'Main Street' was a dirt road that ran alongside a railroad track. A few empty store fronts leaned attentively but appeared to have nothing to say. The same abandoned house he remembered puffed out its grey-streaked cheeks as it continued its slow-motion collapse. The derelict Prairie Lodge Motel sat near the middle of the town, its doors wide open, various pieces of worn, overstuffed furniture dragged out for absent observers to sit on and watch.

Every few months when Dan did an internet search, it came up as a 'ghost town'. He wondered how the people who still lived here—and there were a few of them, tucked away on distant farms or hiding in houses behind closed blinds—felt about that.

'There, there's where it happened,' his mother whispered, tapping the glass gently as if hesitant to disturb him. 'There's where my baby disappeared.'

Dan pulled the car over slowly at this ragged edge of town, easing carefully off the dirt road as he watched for ditches, holes, anything that might trap them here longer than necessary. They'd started much later than he'd planned. First his mother had been unsure what to wear, trying on various outfits, worrying over what might be too casual, what might be 'too much'. Dan wanted to say it wasn't as if they were going to Caroline's funeral, but did not. His mother had put on too much makeup, but when she'd asked how she looked he was reluctant to tell her. The encroaching grief of the day only made her face look worse.

Then she'd decided to make sandwiches in case they got hungry, in case there was no place to stop, and of course out here there wouldn't be. Dan had struggled for patience, knowing that if they started to argue it would never end. It had been mid afternoon by the time they left Denver, meaning this visit would have to be a short one, but it just couldn't be helped.

As soon as he stopped the car his mother was out and pacing in front of the rows of wheat that lapped the edge of the road. He got out quickly, not wanting her to get too far ahead of him. The clouds were lower, heavier, leaking darkness toward the ground in long narrow plumes. He could see the wind coming from a distance, the fields farther off beginning to move like water rolling on the ocean, all so restless, aimless, and, by the time the disturbance arrived at the field where they stood, the wind brought the sound with it, a constant and persistent crackle and fuzz, shifting randomly in volume and tone.

It occurred to him there was no one in charge here to watch this field, to witness its presence in the world, to wonder at its peace or fury. No doubt the owners and the field hands lived some distance away. This was the way of things with modern farming, vast acreages irrigated and cultivated by machinery, and nobody watched what might be going on in the fields. It had been much the same when Caroline vanished. It had seemed almost as if the fields had no owners, but were powers unto themselves, somehow managing on their own, like some ancient place.

Dan took continuous visual notes. He itched to rough these into his typical awkward sketches, but although he always kept sketching supplies in the glove compartment he couldn't bring himself to do so in front of his mother. He never showed his stuff to anyone, but his untrained expressions were all he had to quell his sometimes runaway anxiety.

So, like Van Gogh's 'Wheatfield With Crows', Dan saw long angular shadows carved into the wheat beginning to lift out of their places, turning over then flapping, rising into the turbulent air where they became knife rips in the fabric of the sky.

'She was right here, right here.' His mother's voice was like old screen shredding to rust. She was standing near the edge of the field, her head down, eyes intent on the plants as if waiting for something to come out of the rows. 'My baby was *right here.*'

The wheat was less than three feet tall, even shorter when whipped back and forth like this, a tortured texture of shiny and dull golds. At six, his sister had been much taller. Had she crouched so that her head didn't show? Had she been brave enough to crawl into the field? Or had she been taken like his mother always thought, and dragged, her abductor's back hunched as he'd pulled her into the rows of vibrating wheat?

Out in the field the wheat opened and closed, swirling, now and then revealing pockets of shade, moments of dark opportunity. The long flexible stalks twisted themselves into sheaves and limbs, humanoid forms and moving rivers of grainy muscle, backs and heads made and unmade in the changing shadows teased open by the wind. Overhead the crows screeched their unpleasant proclamations. Dan could not see them but they sounded tormented, ripped apart.

His mother knelt, wept eerily like a child. He had to convince himself it wasn't Caroline. He stepped up behind his mother and laid his hand on her shoulder, confirming that she was shaking, crying. She reached up and laid her hand over his, mistaking his reality check for concern.

A red glow had crept beneath the dark clouds along the horizon, and that along with the increasingly frayed black plumes clawing the ground made him think of forest fires, but there were no forests in that direction to burn—just sky, and wheat, and wind blowing away anything too insubstantial to hold on.

Suddenly a brilliant blaze silvered the front surface of wheat and his mother sprang up, her hands raised in alarm. Dan looked around and, seeing that the pole lamp behind them had come on automatically at dusk, he turned her face gently in that direction and pointed. It seemed a strange place for a street lamp, but he supposed even the smallest towns had at least one for safety.

That light might have been on at the time of his sister's disappearance. He'd been only five, but in his memory there had been a light that had washed all their faces in silver, or had it been more of a bluish cast? There had been Caroline, himself, their mother, and Mom's boyfriend at the time. Ted had been his name, and he'd been the reason they were all out there. Ted said he used to work in the wheat fields, and Dan's mother said it had been a long time since she'd seen a wheat field. They'd both been drinking, and impulsively they took Caroline and Dan on that frightening ride out into the middle of nowhere.

Ted had interacted very little with Dan, so all Dan remembered about him was that he had this big black moustache and that he was quite muscular—he walked around without his shirt on most of the time. Little Danny had thought Ted was a cartoon character, and how it was kind of nice that they had a cartoon character living with them, but like most cartoon characters Ted was a little too loud and a little too scary.

'I never should have dated that Ted. We were all pretty happy until Ted came along,' his mother muttered beside him now. She hadn't had a drink in several years as far as he knew, but like many long time drinkers she still sounded slightly drunk much of the time—drink appeared to have altered how she moved her mouth.

This was all old stuff, and Dan tuned it out. His mother had always blamed ex-husbands and ex-boyfriends for her mistakes, as if she'd been helpless to choose, to do what needed to be done. Just once Dan wished she would do what needed to be done.

When Dan had come here at age fifteen it had been the middle of the day, so this oh-so-brilliant light had not been on. He hadn't wanted to be here in the dark. He didn't want to be here in the dark now.

But the night his sister Caroline disappeared had also been bathed in this selective brilliance. That high light had been on that night as well. No doubt a different type of bulb back in those days. Sodium perhaps, or an arc light. Dan just remembered being five years old and sitting in the back of that smelly old car with his sister. The adults stank of liquor, and they'd gotten out of the car and gone off somewhere to do something, and they'd told Danny and Caroline to stay there. 'Don't get off that seat, kids,' his mother had ordered. 'Do you hear me? No matter what. It's not *safe*. Who knows what might be out there in that field?'

Danny had cried a little—he couldn't even see over the back of the seat and there were noises outside, buzzes and crackles and the sound of the wind over everything, like an angry giant's breath. Caroline kept saying she needed to go to the bathroom, and she was going to open the car door just a little bit, run out and use the bathroom and come right back. Dan kept telling her no, don't do that, but Caroline was a little bit older and never did anything he said.

The only good thing, really, had been the light. Danny told himself the bright light was there because an angel was watching over them, and as long as an angel was watching nothing too terrible could happen. He decided that no matter how confusing everything was, what he believed about the angel was true.

Caroline had climbed out of the car and gone toward the wheat field to use the bathroom. She'd left the car door part way open and that was scary for Danny, looking out the door and seeing the wheat field moving around like that, so he had used every bit of strength he had to pull the car door shut behind her. But what if she couldn't open the door? What if she couldn't get back in? That was the last time he saw his sister.

'I left you two in the car, Dan. I told you two to stay. Why did she get out?'

Dan stared at his mother as she stood with one foot on the edge of the road, the other not quite touching, but almost, the first few stalks of wheat. Behind her the rows dissolved and reformed, shadows moving frenetically, the spaces inside the spaces in constant transformation. He'd answered her questions hundreds of times over the years, so although he wanted to say *because she had to go to the bathroom, you idiot,* he said nothing. He just watched her feet, waiting for something to happen. Overhead was the deafening sound of crows shredding.

There used to be a telephone mounted below the light pole, he remembered. He and his mother and Ted had waited there all those years ago until a highway patrolman came. Ted and his

181

mother had searched the wheat field for over an hour before they made the call. At least that's what his mother had always told him. Danny had stayed in the car with the doors shut, afraid to move.

He guessed they had looked hard for his sister, he guessed that part was true. But they obviously did a bad job because they never found her. They also told the officer they had been standing just a few feet away at the time, gazing up at the stars. What else had they lied about?

The brilliant high light carved a confusing array of shadows out of the wheat, Dan's car, and his mother. His own shadow, too, was part of the mix, but he had some difficulty identifying it. As his mother paced back and forth in front of the field, her shadow self appeared to multiply, times two, times three, more. As the wind increased the wheat parted in strips like hair, the stalks writhing as if in religious fervour, bowing almost horizontal at times, the wind threatening to tear out the plants completely and expose what lay beneath. Pockets of shadow were sent running, some isolated and left standing by themselves closer to the road. Dan could hear wings flapping over him, the sound descending as if the crows might be seeking shelter on the ground.

'She might still be out there, you know,' his mother said. 'I was so confused that night, I just don't think we covered enough of the field. We could have done a better job.'

'The officers searched most of the night.' Dan raised his voice to be heard above the wind. 'They had spotlights, and dogs. And volunteers were out here the rest of the week looking, and for some time after. I've read all the newspaper articles, Mom, every single one. And even when they harvested the wheat that year, they did this section *manually*, remember? They didn't want to damage—they wanted to be careful not to—' He was trying to be careful, calm and logical, but he wasn't sure he even believed what he was saying himself.

'They didn't want to damage her *remains*. That's what you were trying to say, right? Well, I've always thought that was a terrible word. She was a sweet little *girl*.'

'I'm just trying to say that after the wheat was gone there was nothing here. Caroline wasn't here.'

'You don't know for sure.'

'What? You think she got ploughed under? That she's down under the furrows somewhere? Mom, it's been *years*. Something would have turned up.'

'Then she might be alive. We just have to go find her. I've read about this kind of thing. It happens all the time. They find the child years later. She's too scared to tell all these years, and then she does. There's a reunion. It's awkward and it's hard, but she becomes their daughter again. It happens like that sometimes, Danny.'

He noticed how she called him by his childhood name. Danny this and Danny that. It was also the only name Caroline had ever had for him. But more than that, he was taken by her story. To argue with his mother about such a fairytale seemed too cruel, even for her.

He barely noticed the small shadow that had fallen into place not more than a foot or two away from her, a dark hollow shaking with the wind, perhaps thrown out of the body of wheat, vibrating as if barely whole or contained, its edges ragged, discontinuous. At first he thought it was one of the large crows that had finally landed to escape the fierce winds above, ready to take its chances with the winds blowing along the ground, but its feathers so damaged, so torn, Dan couldn't see how it could ever fly again.

183

Until it opened its indistinct eyes, and looked at him, and he knew himself incapable of understanding exactly what he was seeing. If he were Van Gogh he might take these urgent, multi-directional slashes and whorls and assemble them into the recognisable face of his sister Caroline, whose eyes had now gone cold, and no more sympathetic or understandable than the other mysteries that travelled through the natural and unnatural world.

His mother wept so softly now, but he was close enough to hear her above the wind, the hollowed-out change in her voice as this shadow gathered her in and took her deep into the field.

And because he had no right to object, he knew that this time there would be no phone call, there would be no search.

Notes on Contributors

Timothy Parker Russell lives in the Yorkshire Dales and is a sixth-form student. His interests include books, music and participating in motor sport.

Reggie Oliver has been a professional playwright, actor, and theatre director since 1975. His publications include the authorised biography of Stella Gibbons, *Out of the Woodshed*, and five collections of stories of supernatural terror, of which the latest, *Mrs Midnight* (Tartarus 2011) won the Children of the Night Award for 'best work of supernatural fiction in 2011'. Tartarus has also reissued his first collection *The Dreams of Cardinal Vittorini* and will shortly reissue his second collection *The Complete Symphonies of Adolf Hitler*, as well as his latest (and sixth) collection *Flowers of the Sea*. His novel, *The Dracula Papers I: The Scholar's Tale* (Chômu 2011), is the first of a projected four. His stories have appeared in over forty anthologies.

Christopher Fowler is the multi award-winning author of over thirty novels and twelve short story collections including ten Bryant & May mysteries. His collection 'Red Gloves' featured twenty-five new stories to mark his first twenty-five years in print. He recently wrote the 'War of the Worlds' videogame for Paramount with Sir Patrick Stewart, and won the Green Carnation prize for his memoir *Paperboy*. He currently writes for the *Independent on Sunday* and the *Financial Times*. He lives in King's Cross, London.

Rhys Hughes was born in 1966 and began writing fiction from a young age. His first book, the now legendary *Worming the Harpy*, was published by Tartarus Press in 1995. He has published many volumes since then, chiefly collections of short-stories but also a few novels, in several languages.

Mark Valentine's latest books are *At Dusk* (Ex Occidente Press, 2012) and *Selected Stories* (The Swan River Press, 2012). A collection of his tales featuring Ralph Tyler, occult detective (and other stories), *Herald of the Hidden*, is due from Tartarus Press in 2013. He has also written biographies of Arthur Machen and Sarban, and edits *Wormwood*, a journal of the literature of the fantastic, decadent and supernatural.

Anna Taborska was born in London, England. She is an award-winning filmmaker and writer of horror stories, screenplays and poetry. Anna has written and directed two short fiction films, two documentaries and a one-hour TV drama, 'The Rain Has Stopped'. Her stories have been published in a number of anthologies in the UK and the US, and her debut short story collection, 'For Those who Dream Monsters' is due out in late 2013.

John Gaskin, formerly Professor of Naturalistic Philosophy at Trinity College, Dublin, retired in 1997 to travel, 'live more widely', and write stories. Amongst other books he has published two short story collections: *The Dark Companion* (2001) and *The Long Retreating Day* (2006).

Notes on Contributors

Corinna Underwood is a British author who emerges within and without her stories. When she isn't holding a pen you may find her sowing seeds in wild and secret places. www.ambiguousmedia.net

Rosalie Parker grew up on a farm in Buckinghamshire and has now settled in the Yorkshire Dales. Working first as an archaeologist, she has returned to her first love of books, and is a publisher and writer.

Jason A. Wyckoff was born, schooled and lives still in Columbus, Ohio, USA, with his wife and their pets. His first published work is the collection *Black Horse and Other Strange Stories* (Tartarus Press, 2012).

Mark J. Saxton was born in 1967 and lives in the north west of England with his wife, numerous hats and an infinite amount of records and books. A published writer of short fiction and non-fiction, he is currently dabbling in larger, darker projects.

Jayaprakash Satyamurthy lives in Bangalore, India. He is a freelance writer. His short fiction has appeared in *Pratilipi*, *Andromeda Spaceways Inflight Magazine* and the *Lovecraft eZine*.

R.B. Russell is a publisher and writer, living in the Yorkshire Dales. He has had three short story collections published *Putting the Pieces in Place*, *Literary Remains* and *Leave Your Sleep* and a novella *Bloody Baudelaire*).

Stephen Holman was born in Hastings, England in 1962 and migrated to the US in 1984 where he has since had a diverse career as a painter, writer, performance artist and animation director. He has created and designed several children's television series (including 'The Bite-Sized Adventures of Sam Sandwich' for Disney and 'Phantom Investigators' for Warner Bros) and has staged his performance work across the US, Europe and Japan. His art work can be seen on his website: www.stephenholmanart.com

Steve Rasnic Tem is a past winner of the Bram Stoker, World Fantasy, and British Fantasy awards. His two books from 2012 were the novel *Deadfall Hotel* and the noir collection *Ugly Behavior* (New Pulp Press). 2013 will see three new Tem collections: *Onion Songs* (Chomu), *Celestial Inventories* (ChiZine), and *Twember* (NewCon Press).